ALSO BY GILLIAN LINDEN

Remember How I Told You I Loved You?

NEGATIVE SPACE

A Novel

GILLIAN LINDEN

W. W. NORTON & COMPANY
Independent Publishers Since 1923

Copyright © 2024 by Gillian Linden

All rights reserved
Printed in the United States of America
First Edition

For information about permission to reproduce selections from this book, write to Permissions, W. W. Norton & Company, Inc., 500 Fifth Avenue, New York, NY 10110

For information about special discounts for bulk purchases, please contact W. W. Norton Special Sales at specialsales@wwnorton.com or 800-233-4830

Manufacturing by Lake Book Manufacturing
Book design by Anna Oler

ISBN 978-1-324-06554-8

W. W. Norton & Company, Inc., 500 Fifth Avenue, New York, N.Y. 10110
www.wwnorton.com
W. W. Norton & Company Ltd., 15 Carlisle Street, London W1D 3BS

1 2 3 4 5 6 7 8 9 0

For L and S

MONDAY

"DON'T BE SCARED," I said.

Jane was clinging to her stuffed dragon, looking resolved.

"Remember all the candy they give you at the end."

The waiting area was empty, and the receptionist brought us right to the examination room. Jane shoved me off and climbed into the chair. The dentist moved briskly, pulling on gloves and scooting forward on a rolling stool. She wore an herbal perfume that cut through the faintly sweet medical smells of the office. There was a bit of glamour about her, which made me see the trappings of dentistry differently: the turquoise blue lounge chair where Jane sat; the strong light shining onto her face; the silver tools.

She held up Jane's lip and said, "Do you see this? This? Gum infections." She didn't sound interested.

"Huh?" Jane said.

"Infections?" I said. "More cavities?"

"Jane, you're done. You go with Noelle and pick out some treats." When Jane was gone, the dentist said, "Deeper than cavities. Don't worry." She took off the goggles. "If she rinses her mouth with salt water, she won't need the teeth extracted."

"Extracted?"

"I have lots of children rinsing with salt water." She looked up and seemed to be counting them. "Quite a few."

We left, Jane holding a plastic bag with a light-up toothbrush and seven sugar-free lollipops, one for each year of her life. I explained what the dentist had said about the infections, rinsing with salt water.

She said, "I'm not going to do that."

I took her little hand, which moved delicately against my palm, and explained tooth extraction: a strange dentist, a sick feeling from the gas, soreness after.

"Will I cry?" she asked. I told her she would.

That seemed to take care of it. Jane began to sing—*I wake in the morning and I step outside.*

We walked in and out of shade, passing the mother of one of Lewis's classmates. She was wearing a mask and speaking into her phone. *I wake in the morning.* I had to pick up copies of *A Midsummer Night's Dream* for the sixth grade, and I wanted to check in with Jeremy, chair of the English department, about my classes for next year. I was part-time, always the last to find out my schedule, but it was nearly June.

"Look," Jane said, pointing at a tree with its roots exposed; they spread from the trunk like a messy skirt. "Poor tree. Your phone wants something."

"Was that my phone?" There was a reminder on the screen: *Olivia—s.* Something else I had to do. A ninth grader had mentioned suicide in a class discussion about unhappy endings, and the school psychologist had asked me to find out what was behind it. I didn't believe much was behind it, but with suicide you wanted to be sure. Dorothy, the head of school, liked to imagine teachers as guardians, protectors. "Parents have entrusted their children to you," she would say at the beginning of every year. "They are in your care."

We arrived at Jane's school. Jane was singing *hey-ey-ey-ey*, but stopped abruptly when we reached the steps. She pulled a lightly stained mask over her mouth and nose, I hugged her, and she vanished behind the wooden doors.

TWO WOMEN WERE AT the corner and one said, "I don't buy clothes anymore. I have enough to wear until I die." I also, surely, had enough to wear until I died; I had clothes that would outlast me, but I didn't want to dwell on that. I was teaching *The Metamorphosis* and I had to remember what to say and especially what not to say to my class. Teaching made me more aware of everything I didn't know, and it showed me the fragility of the things I thought I did know. Rounding, you'd say I knew nothing about anything.

I wanted to tell my class Kafka was afraid of his father; some of them would certainly relate. Kafka had written a letter about it, and I'd spent the night before annotating my copy, picking out bits to read out loud, providing some context, but this morning I couldn't find it. I checked my folders, the desk, all around the couch, every surface of the apartment. Lewis, who hid my keys and wallet and shoes, said he didn't hide the letter, and Jane said she'd never seen it in her life. "And if you ask me again," she said, "I'm not going to say goodbye to you at school." But I blamed her, Lewis, and Nicholas, and most of all my phone. If I could get more sleep, if I could concentrate, I'd be an organized person, I wouldn't misplace things. And I'd retain information to pass on to my students. Not that they seemed very interested in hearing more from me.

The school building came into view, its bricks patched with sunlight. There was a courtyard in the front, and I stopped there to text the children's babysitter. Lewis had a gardening class after his school and would need a later pickup, and I wanted to let Marian know about Jane and the salt water. There were messages on the screen from Nicholas, in his office for the first time in a year. He'd sent a link to an article about the aftereffects of COVID, which we'd had; a picture of me and Jane in the middle of a snow-covered field; and three requests that I call him, which I did, sitting on the wide steps leading up to the main entrance. The stone was cool against my legs and nearly soft, smoothed by use, like centuries-old linen, which was sturdier and more supple, I'd read, than anything being made today.

Nicholas picked up quickly. "Hello."

"How is it?"

"Depressing. No one's here."

"I thought people had been coming in."

"A few people."

"So what's up?"

"What's up with you?"

"You wanted me to call?"

"I just wanted to say hi. You never respond to texts."

"I didn't hear them."

"Turn the volume up. Hello?"

"Hello?"

"Sorry, that was my work phone. You're here?"

"I'm still here."

"Not you."

Bits of mica in the path glinted at me, and Darya, the movement instructor, walked into the school in her personal atmosphere of eucalyptus and orange. Her name was similar to mine, and occasionally I received an email intended for her. They were mostly dull—questions about attendance, questions about schedules—but once, last year, I was sent a long message from her husband, a chemistry teacher. *Gandhi said forgiveness is a quality of the strong.*

I waved and half stood to go in with her, and remembered Nicholas. "Nicky?" I said.

"I spoke to Paul," he was saying. "Oh. I have to go."

"You have to get off the phone with me?"

"One second," he said, not to me because he hung up.

I texted him a middle-finger emoji. Marian had given my salt-water text a thumbs-up. I put away the phone, feeling discontented. One thing was, I wasn't caring for my children well. I wasn't at ease about the gum infections. "It's unusual to have two at a time," the dentist had said. I wanted to nourish Jane and Lewis. I'd cook tonight—protein and vegetables. I saw minerals pouring into Jane's cells, saw them sparkling like the mica in the ground.

———

THE SCHOOL LOBBY HAD a tiled floor and smelled like cinnamon toast and coffee from the faculty lounge. I'd wondered how
many parents made their pleas during admissions and shelled out
the tuition, higher than the average American salary, because of
the wholesomeness of the smell. I waved to the security guards, all
looking at something on a tablet, and went to the elevator.

My classes, ninth grade and sixth, met in what was called the *rig
room*, off the gym. Floor mats and balance beams were stored here,
and there was a climbing wall. The climbing wall didn't tempt the
ninth graders—it was hard to imagine them climbing anything,
least of all a wall designed for the purpose—but it did intrigue the
sixth graders, especially Jasper. He'd written a poem with the line *I
know the careless mother*. So did I. Jasper's mother, Fiona, was dean
of seventh grade.

The ninth graders wandered in with studied nonchalance. I logged
on to the computer so that my remote students could join on Zoom.

"Rosie," I said, "can you hear me?"

She gave me a thumbs-up. She was sitting outside, and behind
her was a plant with dark, reaching branches. It looked like an
absence rather than a presence, as though it had been cut out of
the fabric of the world.

"Daniel, can you hear me?"

"I can hear you."

Everyone in the room covered their ears. "Not again," Caleb said.

"I can hear you," said Daniel.

"You go, you go," I heard the teacher in the gym next door say.

A tall child came into the rig room and said, "Can you please turn your volume down? We can't hear anything over his voice."

"Can you not hear me?" said Daniel.

"Don't say anything," I said.

"Can you hear me?" Daniel said.

I muted him. "We're going to switch the sound to my laptop." No one would hear Daniel and Rosie except me, and Daniel and Rosie wouldn't hear anyone unless I brought my laptop right next to each speaker. I checked the tabs on my browser and closed a full-body scan relaxation video; I didn't want the students to consider me in relation to the phrase *full body*. I turned off the sound on the classroom computer and found Zoom on my laptop.

It took time. If this had been the sixth grade, the students would have been telling me their weekend plans, and that the room was stuffy, and that I was assigning too much work but the work wasn't as challenging as it had been the year before, when they'd had Ms. Marsh. Some would have draped themselves over the air filter, blocking it completely. Some would have started up the wall. But this was ninth grade, and the students subsided into watchful silence broken by soft laughter.

I opened Zoom, closed Zoom, restarted my computer twice, and finally I was on, and could hear Daniel and Rosie quietly affirm their presence; it was as though they were whispering into my ear. "Can you hear me?" I said.

"Barely," said Daniel.

I held up Kafka's *Selected Stories*, an edition with a yellow cover, powdery under my fingers. "Did everyone remember to bring this?"

A couple of students nodded.

"Hold up your books."

Rosie held up her book and a breeze fluttered the pages. Luca F. put the book on his desk. Several students began to look through their bags. Daniel said, "One second," and his box went black.

"Autumn, do you have this book?" Autumn, a girl with a clear, floating voice that reminded me of Lewis's, gave me a look of pure confusion. Her mother was a corporate lawyer who had asked me pointedly, during a parent-teacher conference, when I would be teaching Shakespeare. Autumn's father was a large man with a brassy cheerfulness. Once I'd run into him just outside the school and he'd said to me, "I can't believe we haven't transferred her yet, you know?"

"That book?" said Autumn.

I nodded.

"I have that book in my bag."

"Can you take it out?" I turned to Ethan. "Do you have this book?"

"It's at my mom's and I spent last night at my dad's." Ethan was supposed to receive two copies of each book.

"I never got that book," said Aimee.

"You did," Luca P. said. "It was in the box at the beginning of the year."

"Oh," said Aimee. "I don't know where that is."

"I didn't get that book," said Philip. "I never got the box, remember?"

I said, "I left the book for you in the office."

He snapped his fingers. "I have to pick it up."

Gabriella, Caleb, and Aria had placed their books on their desks and assumed vague, irritated expressions.

"The book is in my bag," said Hazel, "but I don't know where my bag is. I think I left it in the community gathering space." The community gathering space was in a church, which, like the gym, was being used for classes. My classes had been held there earlier in the year, and sometimes in the rig room, surrounded by rubber and ropes, I longed for the spacious, dark chapel. "Can I go get it?" Hazel said.

"I don't *think* so." I looked at the clock. "We have fifteen minutes left. It's well past time to begin." Relief came into the room, cool and refreshing. "Can you please all remember to bring *this* book next time?

"Franz Kafka was born in Prague, in what was then Bohemia." I looked around, but happily no one seemed eager to know more about Bohemia.

"OLIVIA," I SAID. "Can we please talk?"

Olivia glanced at me and began to pick things up and put them down, moving slowly and without purpose. She lifted a yellow cardigan from the back of her chair, considered it, replaced it; put Kafka in her backpack and took out a floppy planner, opened it, closed it.

Olivia's family had moved to the city from Montreal a few

years ago, but her parents were finalizing their divorce and her father was planning a return to Canada, alone. The grade dean sent an email every few months reminding us that this was all a strain on Olivia. Her father spoke to me bashfully, as though I were a doctor and he was confessing that he still smoked. He spent most of the parent-teacher conference assuring me that he and Olivia's mother remained very close. Her mother, in a separate conference, appeared on my screen huddled in soft-looking shawls. She told me Olivia wasn't doing any work. "Do you know," she said, with wonder and some panic, "I don't think she's read a single book."

Speaking to a parent could be like soothing an anxious pet. I made my voice low and said, "I'm sure we'll be able to get her on track."

"I hope so." Her expression became faintly accusing. "She was a diligent student before all this."

When Olivia was very young, there'd been an accident and she had hurt one of her eyes. In the version of the story Jeremy told me, she and her older sister were playing with sticks, but Darya said she'd tripped in the woods and fallen on a stone. Whatever the cause, her eye changed color from blue to brown, and she couldn't completely see out of it. She parted her hair on the side, and during class it fell in front of her face. Thick and dark, it shielded her protectively, like a bird's wing. It took me a few months to realize that it was her *good* eye she kept covered. All she saw during class was the blurry landscape I navigated when I wasn't wearing my contacts, probably not even that. Nonetheless, if the conversation became broad, detached from the book, she participated. Her work was unbelievably late, but not plagiarized. ("I completely forgot to change the phrasing of that," said Sebastian, explaining his transcription of a LitNotes entry.) I hadn't worried about her before the unhappy-ending class.

I came to regret that class. It was similar to when I'd asked sixth graders to explain away an imagined crime for an *Animal Farm* assignment, and three wrote about burning down the school. I'd emailed the pieces to the grade dean and the school psychologist, and for the rest of the year, every time one of them even alluded to fire, I had to write more emails. After that, when I gave the *Animal Farm* assignment, I told students, *Little things only, no violence.* As if to punish me, they started writing nearly identical pieces about why they'd taken the last slice of pizza. I often found myself reading: *Surely you've heard of the dangers of sodium, comrades?*

The unhappy-ending class started well. I drew hills on the rolling whiteboard to illustrate character arcs. Everyone seemed pleased with the hills, and I enjoyed being up at the board, making diagrams, feeling, for a moment, like a real teacher. The conversation became wide-ranging. Aimee spoke about how artificial endings were in stories.

"But in life," Caleb said, "things really do end."

Gabriella mentioned climate change, the end of the seasons as we know them.

"Maybe the end of humanity," Ethan said.

Aria, who had seemed to be dozing for the first part of the class, looked at me and said, "Endings are just as artificial in life. Our self-absorbed point of view keeps us from seeing—" She brushed her hand through the air. "The ongoing-ness."

Caleb straightened himself and said that not everything was ongoing, and it was kind of hard—harsh—to criticize people for being upset about . . . loss. His expression was odd, vulnerable and pleased with himself.

Aria's face had flushed in an alarming way, and I stepped in. "Different moments pull for different—responses. No one is suggesting anyone should react to anything in any particular way. There aren't rules—there are rules for behavior, not for feelings. I assume everyone knows that, right?"

This plunged the class into apathy, but they quickly started up again, moving in an entirely personal direction. They spoke about things that had gone badly for them, what one of them called their *sufferings and miseries*. Picking up on Caleb's idea, they spoke about loss: pets, friendships, the effects of COVID. "That sounds very hard," I said, a version of which I used several times. There was a girl in the class whose father had died when she was in elementary school. She'd been silent, and I started to notice this and wonder about it. And I was wondering about it when Olivia said, "In certain circumstances, you could understand why a person would want to end things."

The class continued without pause. I thought, *Oh that's fine. I don't have to do anything about that.* But this thought often preceded the belief that I did have to act. When I read the burn-down-the-school stories, I had the same thought, and earlier in the year when I'd asked students to come to class with book recommendations and someone suggested a memoir by a Nazi, or rather a *former* Nazi ("It's really cool to have a window into that way of thinking"), I thought, *They get it, I don't have to follow up.* By the end of the unhappy-ending day, I'd emailed the grade dean and the school psychologist.

Olivia was now before me, gripping her phone. I thought of Jane holding her feathery soft dragon toy at the dentist, how soon Jane, too, would be clinging to a slippery bit of metal and glass. But the dragon was probably coated in flame retardants and other chemicals, toxins even now sinking into her skin. I saw Jane's cells, lacy and weak.

Olivia said, "So."

I looked at her. "Yes. Just who I wanted to speak to." It was such a poor beginning that she gave me a look approaching compassion.

"The other day, when we were talking about endings, you mentioned someone taking his, her, or their own life." I was trying to use only the phrases the school psychologist had given me, which was like hopping on a few mossy rocks to cross a stream. "I wondered how you were thinking about it."

She said, "If things are bad enough and are going to stay bad, you can see how a person would head that way."

I remembered a class I'd taken in college called *Death*. "You were thinking philosophically?"

"Like Okonkwo."

"You were thinking about *Things Fall Apart*?" So she *had* read the book, or was able to seem like a person who'd read the book. I wished her mother were with us.

She didn't reply.

"You were thinking about the end of that novel?"

She had receded into a dream, and her desire not to be in the conversation was something I could feel. Maybe I was feeling my reluctance to press her. I didn't think she was suicidal, but I wasn't completely sure. My great-grandfather had killed himself (*stepped into a well*, my father said, as though this were a distinction), and five years ago my cousin had killed himself. At the school, a child had died by suicide the year I started. These deaths were like a cold pond in the back of my mind.

Like most of my students, Olivia could appear older or younger than she was depending on the day, the hour. Now she seemed tired. She was leaning into the desk and I could imagine her curling up underneath it and falling asleep, as Jane had done once while we were finishing dinner.

I said, "When someone mentions suicide—"

She looked, for a moment, exquisitely bored. "I'm fine."

"If you aren't, there are people to talk to. Me or someone else. I can help you find someone else." ("I try not to just pass the students off," said a math teacher in a meeting about traumatized children. "But," a health teacher jumped in, "sometimes *you* aren't the best person for the job.")

"I'm really fine." She tucked her hair behind an ear so I could see both of her eyes. They watched me patiently.

How, I thought, *do I wrap this up?* I said, "I hope you like Kafka." She smiled, lips closed, and left.

I put my books away with the dispiriting thought that Gregor's death, not entirely not suicide, would allow us to revisit this territory. I wrote to the grade dean and the school psychologist. I couldn't *interpret* the conversation, so I tried to remember Olivia's exact words.

MY EARS WERE SORE FROM the straps of my mask, and my desire for fresh air was a thirst, but I couldn't do anything about it because there was a department meeting. I walked down a flight of stairs and into a room used mostly for history classes, with views of the park, the river, the buildings across the river in Brooklyn. From the upper floors of the school, it all looked pretty and tranquil, like an illustration of a city. The room had a projector, and Glenn from tech was coming to demonstrate a new system for submitting the little essays we wrote about students to explain their grades. The essays, called *narratives*, had until this point been emailed to the administration in single documents; going forward, we would upload them, student by student, to the platform we already used for attendance. And each one would have a word limit.

I checked my texts. Marian had sent a picture of Lewis eating a croissant, and told me Jane was now eager to rinse her mouth with salt water. *She doesn't want the dentist to be mad at you*, she wrote, with a laughing emoji.

Jeremy walked in and sat at the center of the U-shaped arrangement of desks. He took out pink and yellow flyers, elective lists.

"Do we know the word limit?" asked Charlie. He had a PhD and was distantly related to an American president; I couldn't remember which one. His movements were languid, and his conversational style was to oppose whatever anyone else was saying. Sometimes he would pretend he wasn't opposing someone, only to turn on the person definitively. "I know this isn't what you meant," he would say, and then explain why the position, just what the other person meant, was fundamentally wrong and extremely stupid.

Jeremy said, "Glenn says it's not useful to think in terms of word limits, because it's a space issue. It depends on if you're using long or short words."

"There is, in fact, an average?"

"This is really happening *this* year?"

"For years people have said narratives are too long."

Jane had once said, "I wish she was my mother," about a folk-singer at a street fair. This was my feeling about Jeremy: I wished he were my father. He was in his sixties and his face was made of ridges and concavities, like the rough stones Lewis collected. He was skeptical of the students, the school, the idea of education. "What are we even doing here?" he said the year I started. I knew that his informality, his quiet voice, his somewhat frayed clothing were carefully planned, part of an affect he cultivated, and I found this effort touching. He was so *likable*.

"Who has said that?" said Agnes, or Ms. Marsh, the deeply missed teacher of my sixth graders.

"In *these* meetings—you've never heard that?"

"I've never been told that."

"Maybe *your* narratives aren't too long." Jeremy sighed and it was clear a less understanding person would be throwing things, firing someone, or dying of a stroke. And Jeremy had an arrhythmia and had twice suffered—he called them *events*. Both times he'd fully recovered.

"Who makes the decision about the word limit?"

"The platform." Also, we had to change our passwords. The room fell into silence.

"Now you have to announce something really crazy, like we'll have uniforms."

"Mandatory testing."

"Maybe our yearbook photo should show us feeding ourselves into a computer."

Glenn opened the door, and we all started clapping, which had become standard when receiving someone from tech. Technology had rescued the school when in-person instruction wasn't possible, and though in the past tech faculty had been viewed with suspicion by most other teachers, the pandemic had elevated them to a status previously enjoyed only by the mime teacher. But one year in, many of us appeared to have returned to the belief that technology was irritating and pernicious. It demanded too much attention—updates, password changes. It showed us too much of ourselves—the folds in our skin; how our eyes weren't level and one didn't fully open—and not enough of others. The applause for tech now glimmered with irony.

"What is the word limit?" said Charlie as Glenn set up his computer.

"Jenny Berardi," Glenn said, naming the director of communications, "will be sending out an email next week, and it will contain . . ." He stopped, waved his hand like he was fanning away smoke, and seemed to decide against telling us about the email. "More information. I'm only here to demonstrate how you put the narratives into the system."

"Can't you just tell us the word limit now?"

"I'm smart enough to know if I say a word limit and it turns out not to be the right word limit—"

"It'd be fine if your word limit were *under* the real word limit."

Tim peeked at Glenn's screen.

"Don't go by that word count," Glenn said, moving his laptop. "Those are Latin words; they're long. The real word limit will be higher than that."

It became known, without Tim saying anything, that the word count for Glenn's document was 300. Sighs filled the room.

"So the real word limit is 350," said Agnes.

Glenn demonstrated how to put a narrative into the new system, which involved copying it from a template and pasting it into a box on the platform. You had to begin in the template because the platform would not alert you . . .

My feet were cold. I usually discovered at the end of meetings that I had twisted myself up, as if my fingers, arms, and legs were the straw wrappers Lewis folded during a meal, turning them into spirals and pebbles. Next to me, Tim was correcting a set of vocabulary sheets that had the crazed look of notes jotted down at the last moment before fleeing a disaster. Glenn reminded us of the keyboard shortcuts for copy and paste, and said we could go.

"Wait," said Lisa. "Can you explain why we *need* to copy and paste? And where we find the template?"

"Sure." Glenn smiled.

We all sat back down.

I WENT TO THE DEPARTMENT OFFICE to collect myself. Nicholas had texted questions about Jane's gum infections. *Remember when Penny had the gray tooth?* I wrote. The summer before the pandemic, Nicholas's niece's tooth had turned gray, which, we learned, is what happens when a tooth dies. "The nerves died quietly," the dentist had said, explaining how Jane's infections could emerge without any pain. *It's the same,* I wrote. *The dentist said it happens all the time.*

The only other person in the office was Agnes, who had begun working; a copy of *Bleak House* was in her hands. She looked up at me and smiled. "Dickens is so luscious," she said. I smiled back and turned my attention to dinner and reviving Jane's depleted cells. I opened the Notes app on my phone. *Chicken*, I wrote. *Green beans.* That looked short, so I added, *Blueberries.*

I checked my email. The school psychologist had thanked me for the update. Jeremy, whom I cc'd when I wrote to the dean and the psychologist, chimed in. He knew Olivia. She was on the staff of the literary magazine, *Negative Space.* He wasn't concerned. The only thing left was to locate copies of *Midsummer.* Agnes told me there was a set in a fourth-floor classroom.

———

FOUR YEARS AGO, when I started the job, Dorothy had explained to me, "It's not that we *shouldn't* teach Shakespeare." She paused to make sure it was sinking in. "But first we have to ask ourselves, *Should* we teach Shakespeare?" That question and others related to it—how do we teach him? how do we explain why we're teaching him?—came up in meeting after meeting, as we continued to teach him. Certain parents expected it; it was a sign that their children were getting a *quality* education. Other parents saw Shakespeare's presence on reading lists as evidence of the school's retrograde tendencies, its allegiance to a white, male canon. To appease both groups, we saved his plays for the end of the year, and usually didn't ask the students to write essays about them. We gave him time, but not *too much* time. Tim thought of finding a Shakespeare quote to explain his new abbreviated place in the curriculum—something about the passage of years, the inevitability of change. He thought we could circulate it among parents, but he never found just the right one. "Still looking," he'd say cheerfully. There was probably a Shakespeare quote about that, too.

We all loved *Midsummer*. I enjoyed the fairy world, its tiny comforts made of flowers and leaves. I disliked teaching the opening scene, noblemen arguing over the fate of Hermia: marriage, chastity, death. It offended the sixth graders, and could drive them to righteous outbursts.

"Shouldn't it offend them?" Nicholas asked when I told him about it. "Isn't a passionate response what you're going for?"

"I prefer them to stay in their chairs," I said. "But yes. They should be offended. I can enter that space myself."

"Naturally."

"Yes."

"So?"

One former student, a petite boy whose creative writing was exclusively about his fear of boats, had put his finger on the problem. A conversation began about the ways the prejudices described *and expressed* in Shakespeare were still with us, implicated us. The boy said, "But it isn't *our* fault. We're just children. It's not *us*. It's our parents' fault, and other adults." He looked at me, unblinking. "It's not fair that we have to fix it."

"So?" Nicholas said. "He's right about that, too."

"Yes," I said. "But what's that phrase—the sins of the father. We all inherit that."

"Some more than others."

"His framework—we're blameless, you're not. It undermines my authority."

"I wouldn't take it personally." He paused. "Authority, hierarchies—I thought you were against all that. I thought that's why the job was appealing."

"It was not having to give tests. That's what I like."

"Oh right. And the location."

"The location most of all. But you're right, I'm very uncomfortable with authority, especially my own."

"I know."

"I'm not claiming to be an authority—on anything."

"You've been very clear about that."

I thought about it. "But I do need a little authority. For the sake of the class. Everyone likes to feel that someone is steering the ship."

Nicholas said, "Some people are only happy when *they're* the ones steering, like Jane."

"Maybe this boy is like Jane." I felt myself soften toward him. If his writing were to be believed, he kept getting dragged out onto the ocean, had spent many hours at sea, wet, hungry, and cold. "The thing is," I said, "not having a hierarchy only works if they *listen* to me."

ON THE FOURTH FLOOR I passed two high school students in a nest near the stairs: notebooks, headphones, shiny bags of potato chips. Their slim arms shuffled papers, and one of them was humming quietly. I stopped in the office to say hello to Irene, head of the middle school.

"I haven't seen *you* in a long time," she said. "How's Marty?"

I said, "Those goddamn scones." Marty ate scones and muffins all through class, flouting pandemic rules. "And he's playing video games on his laptop."

Irene rolled her eyes. "Peg said Jonas was doing that."

"Jonas, yes," I said. "Maybe Jasper."

"Come by tomorrow, will you? We can talk."

I waved and made my way to 405, stopping to look in the window before opening the door. The room was occupied. Jeremy was half sitting on the desk, and next to him, in a posture mirroring his, was Olivia. They looked like a pre-pandemic image from a school brochure, knees and hands almost meeting, bent over a piece of paper that seemed to have a poem written on it. *Negative Space*, I thought, surprised that Olivia was involved enough to meet with the faculty coordinator after school. It wasn't just their closeness that recalled earlier times; they weren't wearing masks. Olivia had clear skin, and the curve of her jaw was gentle, nearly plump. She looked very young, and not a bit tired. They weren't supposed to be alone in the room with the door closed; this rule had been put in place two years ago—to protect the faculty, we were told. Well, many of the older teachers viewed the rules as a menu from which they chose what suited them.

I looked past them to the bookshelves for copies of *Midsummer*, which would be a row of narrow gray spines, but I was distracted by a movement at the desk. When I looked back, his hand was on her shoulder. He moved his head to touch hers. *It's fine*, I thought. *It's a fatherly gesture.* When I was in high school, teachers had touched me. Men and women had hugged me, ruffled my hair. One history teacher who was around Jeremy's age had traced a line on my cheek, showing me the placement and length of his son's skateboarding scar. Things were different now, but Jeremy had spent most of his career in that other time, when not all touch was transgressive. *I don't have to do anything about this*, I thought.

I knocked and opened the door, and they floated apart.

"I'm looking for *Midsummer*s," I said, feeling clumsy and intrusive, as I had when, searching for tech support, I'd walked into an after-school cello lesson. "Hi, Olivia."

"Not here, I don't think. Try 503." Jeremy was smiling with

what seemed like some private irony. *She* was looking at me as though she'd never seen me before in her life.

"Sorry," I said. "Sorry. See you tomorrow."

OUTSIDE IT HAD GROWN WARMER, and the pale leaves were glittery on the trees. Teenagers were lounging in a showy way on the steps of the church. One was holding a guitar; he didn't look like he was thinking of playing it. When I was half a block from the school, I started calling people: first Nicholas and my friend Jessica, who didn't pick up, and then my mother, who did.

"Hi," she said.

I said, "I've had a bad day."

"Tell me about Jane's teeth."

"No, it's not that. The dentist said that happens all the time."

"It happened to you," my mother said somberly, and began the story of my childhood tooth extraction. "Your cheek was *swollen* . . ."

"Yes."

" . . . and an abscess."

"I know."

" . . . and rushed to the dental surgeon."

"Jane shouldn't need the teeth removed. The dentist said they'll just fall out."

"Oh?"

"The body rejects them."

"Well. That sounds good then."

"I'm not saying it's good she has gum infections." I wanted my mother to believe that the problem of Jane's teeth, while not negligible, was not very big. But I saw she was going to linger on the possibility that the problem *was* very big, could bloom into a crisis. "The dentist said it would be fine," I said, feeling weak, as I had when I'd told Olivia, *I hope you like Kafka.*

"OK," my mother said.

"You don't sound like you think it's OK."

"Lovey." She paused. "How do I know? I wasn't at the dentist with you."

"I'm telling you what the dentist *said.*"

"And I'm saying OK."

"But I don't think you really think it's OK."

"You told me that Jane has two gum infections. You said *you* don't think it's good. I don't know what I can say."

"You're right." The tag on my bra was itching. "I'm sorry."

"Are *you* OK?"

"Yes." I was standing outside the grocery store. "I have to go."

EVEN WHEN I WAS MISERABLE, the organic grocery store filled me with hope. Here were some of my favorite things: crackers made entirely of seeds, clamshells of emerald spinach, glass jars of yogurt printed with the names of the farm's cows. In the store I forgot that even the cardboard packages were laced with microplastics that would stay in my children's bloodstreams for the rest of their lives. I forgot that the dairy industry was a major contributor to climate change, and that some people thought cows didn't enjoy being constantly milked. I put a bag of pre-washed green beans into my crate, along with lemon cookies, blueberries, a loaf of white bread called *French Sourdough*. Even in this environment, the Styrofoam packages of raw chicken were unappetizing, but I put one in an extra plastic bag and went to check out.

I carried my groceries home. The spring air was clear, mild. I was beginning to sweat from the weight of the food, my computer, my books, and my mind felt stale. When I reached my building, I put the bags down on the stoop and called Nicholas again.

"You really think her gums are OK?" he said.

"I don't know. I have no idea. I need to talk to you. I saw something." I described Jeremy and Olivia, the contact between them.

"Is she the one with the funny eyes?"

"You barely notice it. But yes, that girl."

"And what is Negative Space?"

"The *literary magazine*. But I don't know that it was a meeting. They were the only ones there. It's late in the year to be reviewing submissions."

"Their heads touched?"

"It could have been a gesture of support. A way of providing comfort."

"You always said he was like a dad."

"I wouldn't dream of touching a student like that." I saw how this could be the problem. Other teachers still gave students hugs, grasped their hands to help them stand up. I became uncomfortable if a student sat too close to me, if I thought I had looked at one of them for too long. If I were more relaxed, maybe I wouldn't have seen anything out of the ordinary in that room. I thought, *I really don't need to do anything about this.* The loveliness of the afternoon—the sparkly leaves, the gently rocking shadows on the building across the street—seemed to draw closer, to pull me in. I thought, *Everything is fine.*

"Do you think it could be nothing?" I said.

"I don't know," said Nicholas. "I wasn't there. You just said you'd never touch a student that way."

"But no. No. Don't go by that. I'm so generally uncomfortable. I'm so paranoid."

"You said they separated when you walked in."

"I probably surprised them."

"Exactly," he said. "You should talk to someone."

"The person I talk to at school is Jeremy."

"Someone else, obviously."

The tag again. I scratched my ribs. "I have to go," I said. "I have to take over from Marian."

"OK," Nicholas said. "I'll be late tonight."

"Right."

"OK, thanks. Take care."

"Take care?"

He laughed, lowered his voice. "I'm at *work.* I have to go now, too."

"Fine," I said. "Bye."

———

I OFTEN THREW TANTRUMS, one after another, in my head. I meant to keep them there, but little pieces would leak out. I'd be short on the phone with my mother, I'd yell at Nicholas or the children. Alone in the bathroom I'd make crazy faces at the mirror or make my hands into fists and shake them at nothing. I didn't like these leaks, even when they happened in the privacy of the bathroom. They showed me how wretched it was to be in the grip of what the child psychologist at Lewis's school called *big feelings*. But they should have made me sympathetic to my children's tantrums. They should have given me some idea of how to assuage them, at least how to avoid making them worse.

Marian, leaving the apartment, said Lewis was so tired he could barely stand. It would have been wise to make him a peanut butter sandwich and put him to bed, but I was thinking of Jane's cells. I pounded the chicken breasts with a rolling pin, pressed them into bread crumbs, fried them in oil. I simmered water and placed a metal steamer basket full of green beans over it. I brought a footstool next to me where Lewis could watch, which he did, swaying in his fatigue and nearly falling over twice, until he reached out, touched the pot. Screamed.

I held him, patted his back, checked his palm for a blister. When he was quiet, I brought him to the couch, where Jane was watching a cartoon about an otter, which, she claimed one evening, had taught her everything she knew. And whenever I asked her, "Where did you learn that?" she'd say, "The otter show." Lewis didn't want to sit and watch TV. As I finished cooking, he dragged chairs around the living room and took most of the cushions off the couch.

During dinner, he wanted to stand on his chair. When I asked him to sit down, and tried to bribe him with dried cherries, and finally threatened him, he pushed his plate across the table and knocked over my water glass. I began to yell and he ran to the coffee table, stood on top of it, and screamed, his face the colors of a sunset. I carried him into his bedroom, as he kicked and struggled, and tried to shut the door because, I told him, he would be safer there; there were more soft places. He threw himself backward, headfirst, onto the thin rug, not actually so soft. I thought, *Why haven't I found a thicker rug for this room?* I thought, *What I need to do is cover this room in pillows.* He screamed. I was shouting: *What are you doing? You're hurting yourself.* Jane was shouting, too: *I'm scared. I'm scared.*

I wasn't scared for Lewis, but I hoped the neighbors wouldn't call Child Protective Services because of the noise. I picked him up. *Shhhh*, I said. *Poor you. You feel so bad.* He sobbed against me, and I ushered him through his bedtime routine, with Jane back on the couch in front of her show with a notebook and pencil, drawing mazes for the otter.

"What makes them otter mazes?" I asked.

"They're set in outer space," she said.

"Sorry, Mama," Lewis said when he was in his bed and I'd turned out the light.

"What for?" I put my head against his arm, warm and smooth like shallow water.

"All the screaming," he said, and fell asleep.

Jane rinsed her mouth with salt water and I read her a story about a doll whose child owner decides she's sick and gives her medicine, something sticky that collects behind her eyes, gluing them shut. When the child leaves the nursery, the other toys wash away the medicine, curing the doll of *the only ailment she had ever had.*

"That was strange," Jane said. "Mom, I'm afraid of death again."

"Let's talk about it in the morning," I said.

"I'm afraid I won't be able to talk to you when I die. I can't stand it."

We were in her bed, across the room from Lewis, deeply asleep, as he almost always remained through Jane's story and our conversations. The low reading light didn't seem to bother him. But if Jane became very loud, he would wake up.

"We can't disturb your brother," I told Jane. "I know you're scared. Remember what we've said about this?"

"No," she said. "I don't remember."

"I can't go through *everything* now. But it's not something you need to worry about for a long time."

"But will I be able to talk to you?" she said.

"Very smart people have thought a lot about death—they have spent their lives studying it—and they think it's OK. They aren't afraid."

"But I want to know if I'll be able to *talk* to you."

"I don't think so," I said.

She gasped.

"But I don't know."

"So I might be able to talk to you?"

"Let's talk about it in the morning."

"So I might be able to talk to you?" she said again.

"I don't know, no one knows."

She fell asleep.

I LAY ON THE COUCH, blue and vast. A chiropractor had told me the couch was the source of all of my physical complaints, which made collapsing into it more pleasurable, an act of defiance. I checked my email, hoping to find Jeremy had written with an explanation, a confession, something that took the matter off my plate, as earlier he'd minimized Olivia's suicide comment. But there was nothing.

I went to the kitchen to get cookies and picked up the biography I was reading of Elizabeth I. Here was a woman with a lot on her plate, and it was comforting to bring her to mind, a powerful woman, the opposite of Olivia. Thinking about *her* broke my warm feelings about the couch and the book into dry fragments. The cookie tasted of its plastic carton. I switched to a book that argued that you could wash every single garment you owned— even wool, even cashmere—at home, in water. I took the book to bed and waited for the words to lift and float, cross each other, like toys bobbing in Lewis's bath. I fell asleep.

Sometime later Nicholas came into bed next to me, with headphones in his ears and a sitcom from the nineties playing on his phone. "It smells good," he said.

"What?"

"The apartment smells good."

"I cooked chicken cutlets," I said. "I wanted—" He was watching his show.

"Yes?" he said.

I took out one of his earphones.

"You wanted what?" he said.

"I thought they needed to eat something healthy," I said.

"You made fried chicken?" he said.

"It wasn't *deep* fried. Can you turn over?" I pushed his shoulder so he turned away from me. "Your phone is too bright."

But now I was up, my mind alert. I tried to picture Jeremy's expression when his head met Olivia's. Had it been caring? Solicitous? *Coaxing? Had* it been coaxing? I couldn't recall her face in that moment at all. His head blocked hers, or I'd looked away. The next time I fell asleep, the change was abrupt, like passing from a room flooded with light into a windowless closet, completely dark.

TUESDAY

I WOKE UP while it was still dark and put the soap dish on the kitchen table, next to my laptop. I was writing about things in my apartment. Sometimes I wrote about the same object for a few days in a row, sometimes I switched, a new one each day, sometimes I returned to something I'd already written about a month or so earlier. I'd made the mistake of describing what I was doing to Nicholas, who later, during a fight, called it solipsistic. Most recently he'd asked, "Is it some kind of therapy?"

"No," I said. "Why would you say that?"

"You said it was soothing."

"It's soothing," I said, "because it's engaging. But that isn't the point."

"What's the point?"

I didn't know the point *yet*. I thought a pattern might emerge.

The soap dish was gritty to touch and had a chip on the edge from when Lewis dropped it in the sink. There were a few pieces of a translucent blue bar soap in it, something Nicholas had brought back from a hotel, when he still traveled for his job. We had a box half full of soaps wrapped in tissue paper, small bottles of perfumed lotion. When Nicholas returned to traveling, the box would fill up again. I was picking up the dish to see if there was any mark on the bottom when Lewis and Jane woke up.

The first thing they did in the morning was take showers, a habit begun after Jane had pinworms for the third time. "Will the mama pinworm be mad at me for hurting her babies?" she asked when she first drank the medicine. "She won't know who's done it," I told her.

I escorted Jane out of the water, wrapping a towel around her, and held Lewis's hand as he stepped into it. I dressed and fed them—cream cheese on a miniature bagel, yogurt with honey, apple slices, cut-up grapes. Nicholas was in the bathroom, shaving his head. "You aren't going to like this," he'd said upon waking, "I have a call at seven thirty." He trotted from the bathroom to our bedroom, where he'd set up an office—a flimsy desk and chair, a computer that whirred and murmured day and night, like a creature settling and resettling into a nest. He wouldn't shut it down because of the time it took to start up. "When are you dismantling this?" I'd asked him recently, pointing to the arrangement. "Am I dismantling it?" he'd said.

Lewis laid his apple and grape pieces in a pattern around the corner of the table. I took a picture with my phone and put it in my bag with copies of Elizabeth Bishop's "The Fish." I'd decided to read the poem with the sixth grade and let the class drift into anecdotes about nature. The students could fill any amount of time talking about their country houses: leaky roofs, bears getting into the garbage, deer tearing up the gardens.

Jane put her plate in the sink and described her dream. "My friend said, *A nurse is going to take the word bird from your body, and it is going to hurt.*"

"Which friend?" I said.

She ignored the question. "I didn't feel scared in the dream, but I did when I woke up. Do you understand?"

"I do," I said. "No one is going to hurt you."

"I know that," she said.

My ninth-grade class didn't meet on Tuesdays, which was helpful; I didn't want to see Olivia. It had come to me that I should place the matter in the hands of the faculty advisor, Robin. She had thin, pale lips and a graceful way of moving her hands through the air as she spoke. After meeting with her, I would find myself doing the same, and performing her other mannerisms— nibbling my lip; drawing my fingers along my cheekbone—as though her influence were a drug I was slow to metabolize. She was also undermining, and in copying her gestures, I felt I was abasing myself, but sometimes she would seem pleased with me and this gave me a thorough sense of belonging. Though I knew it was in my interest to avoid her, I sometimes sought her out, and when I thought of speaking with her about Jeremy, I had a feeling of anticipation that was separate from the question of his behavior.

I put jackets on Lewis and Jane. Jane said, "How many Lewises are there in your class, Lewis?"

"Two," Lewis said. "But there's only one me."

"Let me look at your mouth, Jane," I said.

"Not *now*."

"Just let me see." I pulled her lip up. The two bumps sat neatly over each infected tooth like little maroon clouds. The teeth themselves were to my eyes still perfect—shiny surfaces, clean sharp edges. "They're OK," I said.

Jane said, "Can I put my mask back on?"

JANE AND I BROUGHT LEWIS to his playground for early drop-off. Before school began, the playground was attended by *floaters*, fresh young people who seemed unburdened, easeful, though whether they were either of those things I didn't know. They were auditioning for full-time employment at the school, considered a desirable place for students and teachers. It was in an old mansion made of cool gray limestone. Tulips and magnolias blossomed in the front garden in the spring, and more magnolias and a large maple shaded the playground. Lewis's teachers explained language acquisition and social development, and sent home stapled packets of paintings and collages. They knew us, the parents, and didn't seem to despise us. The head of school had hugged me when my mother started chemotherapy. The tuition was high, not as high as at the school where I taught, but Nicholas and I could just afford it. We thought it was worth it, which was probably what the parents of my students thought.

Lewis went straight into the playground and stood near the fence. He was silent; his silence when we were on the grounds of his school was a cloud that enveloped him, constraining his movements so that he walked stiffly.

"Goodbye, Lewis," I said.

He turned and brought his hand up in a frozen wave.

At the drop-off at Jane's school, which was public, there were no floaters. Children darted around parents, grabbed arms and said they were hungry, tired, and extremely thirsty. They dropped their backpacks wherever. The main thing was to remember to give Jane her lunch. When I forgot and left it with the security guard, Jane had to walk to what she grimly referred to as *the office* to retrieve it. It was a long walk and she worried she'd get lost, ending up not at *the office*, she said, but *just anywhere*.

"Here," I said, handing her the metal box with her sandwich and carrots.

"It's too heavy." But she took it.

Jane's teacher called from a side entrance, and children surged toward her in a flutter of pastel clothing, sequins, reflective patches, little toys bobbing from their wrists and backpacks.

"Bye, Jane," I called.

She looked to me, smiled underneath her mask, and was gone.

AT MY SCHOOL I WENT first to the faculty lounge. A history teacher, a man with a light bearing, as though he were only partially affected by gravity, was buttering a slice of toast. I brought my things to the far corner of the room, where there were paned windows on both sides. I liked knowing that only some squares of glass separated me from the street. I liked seeing the people walking by, people who thought nothing of the school; it was just a building they passed on their way to someplace else.

Jeremy walked up to me right as I took out my phone; I hadn't noticed that he was in the room.

"Did you find the *Midsummers*?" He perched on a stool, looking not monstrous at all in a green sweater and canvas shoes. He didn't gleam like the history teacher, but he was pleasing, like a thoughtfully constructed cabinet. Maybe it wasn't so much that I wanted to be his child as I wanted to be him. Did that amount to the same thing?

"No," I said.

"Did you check 503?"

"No." I saw a questioning expression begin around his eyes. "I'll look this morning."

"Because that's where they are." His voice was sharp, but his face quickly relaxed. "Next year," he said.

"Sorry?"

"Your classes."

"Oh right. I've been meaning to ask."

"I don't know anything yet."

"Oh."

"I just didn't want you to think I'd forgotten."

He had sought me out and was aimlessly extending the conversation. It was enjoyable to observe him fishing; it gave me a feeling of control. But if I wanted that feeling to continue, I couldn't be drawn in to speaking about Olivia. I began to pack up my things, slowly to avoid the impression I was fleeing.

"Olivia," Jeremy said, putting his hand on my shoulder and raising his eyebrows as if to say, *What a mess*. It wasn't the first time he'd touched me. He was what is called a *physical* person, as if you could be any other kind. He often patted my arm or hand or knee when making a point. It was one of the things I liked so much about him. It wasn't creepy; it expressed, I thought, the right kind of affection and warmth. I thought, *Affection. Warmth.* Surely we weren't trying to eliminate those desirable feelings and their physical—*physical*—manifestations? Surely . . . (*Surely you've heard of the dangers of sodium, comrades?*)

"Yeah," I said. "Olivia."

"Did Tonya tell you what's been going on?" Tonya was the school psychologist.

"The divorce," I said. "COVID. Olivia made that comment in my class."

"The suicide comment."

"We were talking about unhappy endings," I said. "Who knows why anyone says anything."

"Yes," he said. "I don't think that's something to worry about."

"Me neither."

"No. More than the divorce. Did Tonya tell you?"

I shook my head.

"I'm not supposed to say."

His voice was low, and I had to lean close to hear him. He had a bracing chemical smell, the scent of a popular deodorant, which Nicholas used as well. There'd been a study linking some of the brand's products to cancer in rats, and a partial recall had been ordered. "Hang on," Nicholas had said. "Just hang on." He'd tapped at his phone as I reached for it, then held it up. "See? It's

43

fine." The recall had been for aerosols, which he didn't use. But everything learned on the phone was provisional; you could discover anything on the phone—reassuring news, more often troubling news. Had Nicholas pursued a different search, he'd have learned that all deodorants, not just aerosols, not just his brand, cause cancer, and not just in rats. The phone was like the children's toy baskets, in which I'd find the felt doll Lewis had lost, and also dried-up clementine peels, a toothbrush with darkened bristles, a watch face missing its strap.

"What's going on?" I said to Jeremy, my voice low too.

"I can't say much." He put his hand over his mouth as though to prevent words from getting out. "It has to do with her uncle."

"Her uncle."

"Mother's brother," he said. "She's been *confiding* in me. Well, can you imagine talking to Tonya?"

"*I* try not to. Does Tonya know?"

"She knows. It'll be in the news. They've been trying to keep it out."

I wanted to hear exactly what was happening with Olivia's uncle, but I needed to end the conversation. Jeremy was confiding in me, and now I had joined him in insulting the school psychologist, and if we continued talking, I'd insult more and more people at the school. It was another leak; when I had a receptive audience, I'd complain about every single person I worked with.

Each year we had to watch videos about harassment and abuse, and Tonya would sometimes come to a department meeting to explain our responsibilities when it came to things we saw, things

44

students revealed, intentionally or not. It could be bruises, the absence of a helmet when biking to school a few days in a row, a few lines in a short story. We were legally culpable if we knew of a situation and did nothing. Jeremy and Olivia alone in the room, Jeremy leaning his head into hers, like a cat nudging his nose against someone for a pat. There didn't need to be anything more than that; the room and the nudge were more than enough. And here I was with Jeremy, behaving in a companionable way.

"I have to go," I said. "I have to teach."

He looked at his watch, frowning.

"I have to get there early. You know how I am."

The reminder of how I was seemed to reassure him.

"Sure," he said.

When I stood, my wallet fell and coins tumbled across the floor. In spite of finding it intolerable, finding nothing funny about it, I often enacted the cliché of a scattered woman, a mother of young children. Jeremy didn't try to make me laugh. He said, "I hate it when that happens," and knelt to help me pick them up.

THE RIG ROOM SEEMED MISTY and had a rancid smell. I put my bag on the table and checked my phone. Marian had sent a picture of Lewis pressing his finger into a blueberry muffin and said he wanted a hot dog for lunch. *Sounds good*, I wrote. Nicholas had read that every hot dog you ate subtracted fifteen minutes from your life, but I wasn't in the mood to connect frightening health news to my children.

My sixth graders came in. They still moved quickly, in little bursts, like Jane and her classmates, but by the time they were in ninth grade this would change: their motions would become smoother and heavier, considered. When I thought of Jane or Lewis developing more embellished self-consciousness, I felt anticipatory grief. In my students, I was grateful for any amount of containment.

Peter turned to Lily and said, "Tell her what happened." They avoided my name; I was *her* and *you* and the blank space after *excuse me* or *um*.

"What happened?" I said, ready to send Lily to the nurse. The younger students often needed tending. They had headaches and became very tired. They lost teeth, something I found slightly revolting even when it happened to Jane.

"I'm fine." Lily was restlessly tugging at her jersey. She was, as usual, dressed in her soccer uniform. Her father had told me that she played in a competitive league and was a nonreader.

"Oh?"

"She doesn't like books. Never has. So."

Many parents used conferences to make sweeping assertions about their children. Aria had a photographic memory. Ethan had read twenty books during the first two months of the pandemic. Louisa was unimaginative in a clinical sense, had been born without the capacity. Austin despised authority figures, obviously including teachers. These facts were laid out with a hard, bright expression, as if to say: *What do you think about* that?

Lily was rubbing her hands together.

"Tell her," Peter said.

"Are you cold?" I said.

"It was chilly in Mr. Cote's class." A few of them laughed.

I said, "What's going on?"

"I got in trouble in Mr. Cote's class." Lily was scratching her leg. "He made me sit in front of the fan for a while."

"For the whole class," said Peter.

"It's fine," Lily said.

"That's how he is," Piper said. "He's just *like* that."

Like cruel? Like sadistic?

"Once he threw a book at me," said Jasper. He smiled.

"Lily," I said, "do you want to go to the nurse to see if she has a heating pack?"

"I don't think she has that. It's not a big deal."

"Does anyone have an extra layer for Lily?"

Aurora took a blue sweatshirt out of her bag and handed it to me.

"OK." I passed along the sweatshirt. "I brought in a poem."

WITH THE NEWS THAT Mr. Cote might be torturing his students, I had two things to tell the faculty advisor, but since having Lewis, I'd discovered two could be emotionally simpler than one. When I was angry and felt driven to explain how the noise, the mess, the impediments to concentration were ruining my life, if I addressed myself to both children, the interaction was diluted, and I didn't suffer much guilt afterward.

Speaking with Robin about Jeremy and Mr. Cote, Emile

Cote, would be easier than speaking with her about Jeremy alone. I'd start with Emile, what the students had said, then describe what I saw with Jeremy. I'd tell it all in a straightforward way, as though I were reading from a home appliance manual. *She* could interpret it. I'd wondered about her title, *faculty advisor*. Was she an advocate or some kind of minder? It seemed her job had to do with human resources—the phrase made me think of a morgue. Well, human resources was meant to sort out this kind of thing, exactly this. She could be as hard to locate as Olivia, but today that wasn't a problem, because there was a New Faculty Meeting this afternoon, the last of the year, and she would be leading it.

NEW FACULTY MEETINGS WERE HELD in the basement, in a room used to store projectors and screens. For the meetings, chairs were placed in a semicircle, and a music stand was used as a podium. The room was washed with flat, fluorescent light and had a gloomy clarity. Half windows near the ceiling showed the feet of people walking by. I trained my eyes on them, but the view was not as consoling as the one from the faculty cafeteria.

New Faculty was a roomy category, extending to teachers who had been at the school for six years, though most of them didn't attend meetings. Administrators did attend, and today the room was three quarters full. Jeremy wasn't there, but Darya and Tonya were sitting in the front row, each absorbed in a phone. I chose a spot near the door.

Robin walked to the music stand and was clearing her throat. She was wearing velvet heels and a fitted skirt, the kind that Jane had asked me to get her.

"Like this," she'd said, gathering her dress so that it clung to her legs.

"It's harder to move in tight clothes," I told her.

"I don't care about that," she said.

Robin's assistant, Miles, stood to the left and just behind her, holding a stack of printed paper. *He* once told me he tried to exist on as few calories as possible, a longevity practice.

"I'm amazed," he said, "but I'm trying to live *longer*."

"I think we'd all hope to live just the right amount of time," I said.

He gazed at me silently and turned back to his body. "If I could get a little more emaciated," he said, frowning at his midsection, "I'd be exactly where I wanted."

If Miles had been a student, he'd generate streams of emails to grade deans, department chairs, the school psychologist. I didn't want to wish him luck, so I just said, "I'd miss bagels."

Robin was smiling under her mask. Her eyes were dark. As the room became quiet, her focus shifted among us. She held a tiny cup of wine.

It was the last meeting of the year. Robin reminded us to submit narratives in a timely manner, and stressed the importance of not surprising parents. "Anything *critical* should have already been communicated by a grade dean or department head. When the parent comes across it in the narrative, it shouldn't be a shock."

I'd gleaned that a parent reading criticism of his child should be like Lewis encountering the scary part of a children's book for the fifth or sixth time. *Oh yes, I remember this*, he might think. *I've seen it before. It doesn't end terribly.*

"Think about how what you say will *land*," Robin said. "And be brief. Get in, get out, move on to the next."

She made it sound orderly and satisfying, like organizing the cutlery drawer, which wasn't my experience. You were meant to describe what was best in a child, but sometimes that wasn't evident in class, and then you had to *imagine* what it could be, write about that. *But* a handful of the students were really perceptive, thoughtful, and creative, and how did you convey the shift from fiction to fact? I extravagantly praised the smart children. For everyone else, I picked a scrap—half a line of a poem, a simple observation made in class—and interpreted it broadly, mining it for insights that might or might not be there.

Robin was speaking about students who didn't participate. "There are many ways of being quiet," she said. "For example, is the child *attentively* quiet?"

Tonya stood up. "You might think about a child's posture. Yes? Are they looking at the other students? But if they aren't, they may be daydreaming."

"And we know how valuable daydreaming is," said Robin.

"If you're having trouble getting started, you can describe the way a student enters the room, takes out her books . . ."

A weightless feeling came over me. I was hungry.

Robin said, "It's not the *student's* job to communicate. It's the teacher's job—you all know this—it's the teacher's job to discover how to draw out a student."

I thought of Lewis's circumscribed wave, his quietness that was like fog. He'd come home the other day and reported that he was skipped over again in some sharing activity.

"Lewis," Jane said, "you have to *say* something."

"You say something," Lewis said to me. "Say something to my teacher."

"I'll say you were upset you were skipped."

"No," he said. "Not I was *upset*. Just I was *skipped*."

I LINGERED AT THE END of the meeting, folding my jacket and looking through my bag. "Bye," Darya said as she left. I opened the *Times* on my phone. The news was very bad: COVID, white supremacists, climate change.

I waited for the room to thin out, empty. It was five o'clock, and I was due home at five thirty. I texted Marian that I might be a few minutes late. She wrote back, *ok*, and I understood that it wasn't *really* OK. When there were only a few people left, I moved closer to Robin and tried to catch her eye. Miles intercepted my look.

"Can I help you with something?" he said.

"I need to speak to Robin," I said. "I have a situation. Two, actually."

"Uh-oh."

"Yes."

"Something going on?" Robin said.

―――

ROBIN HAD ALLERGIES, and even before COVID she'd kept two air filters running in her office. There was no carpet or uphol-stery, and the windows were perfectly clean, so the room had the quality of an in-between space—a balcony, a screened porch. In one corner, a standing lamp with a paper shade glowed like some-thing soft and porous from the galaxy. The office was cool, and offered visitors only what looked like an old church pew. Rob-in's chair was spare, with a thin, flat seat and a delicate back. She seemed like the kind of person who didn't need, didn't even want, comfort. I sat on the pew, tried to stack my things next to me, but they overflowed to the floor. I made them into a pile by my feet, feeling slovenly.

"Do you mind?" Robin removed her mask, and took out a legal pad, put it to the side. "So? Aimee's dad again?"

A couple of months ago we'd had what the school called a *neces-sary uncomfortable moment* in the ninth grade while discussing *The Fire Next Time*. Aimee had said something like, *Well, fortunately things have changed since Baldwin wrote this*, and before she was through speaking, several hands went up. Things hadn't changed much. Not enough. *Look around you*, Eloise said. Some students actually did look around, but most were familiar with the point: nearly everyone in the rig room was white.

I described what happened later the same day in an English department meeting, which sometimes began with Jeremy asking if anyone had any *N. U. M.*'s to report. He would pause for a moment before and after the initials to highlight his critical stance, though the exact target of his criticism—was it just the euphemistic language or did he object to the amount of attention paid to these issues?—I never knew. That night Aimee's father wrote to say his daughter was upset because her classmates had accused her of racism.

Robin, Jeremy, and I met with Aimee's father, an attorney named Benjamin, the following week. Coming in, he'd been quite resolute, but as we spoke he seemed to grow worried that in defending Aimee too strongly *he* might be seen as racist. He changed tacks, expressing his displeasure that Aimee's classes were so white, and explaining how much he valued diversity, which was among the reasons he'd wanted to live in the city. He asked what he could do to help the school become a more equitable institution.

Jeremy was expressionless, and he remained silent as Robin began to speak about admissions efforts that were changing the composition of the student body.

"In the lower grades, the picture is already very different," she said.

But with the turn of subject away from him, Benjamin's interest flagged, and the discussion petered out.

"NOTHING ABOUT AIMEE," I said to Robin, whose face relaxed. "No. But in my sixth grade, Lily came to class shivering. Mr. Cote—Emile—had made her sit in front of a fan. It sounded like a punishment."

Robin smiled dryly. "Listen, there's a whole situation there."

"Oh?"

"I can't say anything." She sighed. "Don't repeat this."

"I won't," I said.

"Do you know him?"

"I had a meeting at the beginning of the year with him and Irene. He didn't really talk."

"Some people love him. He's an acquired taste. Was that it?"

I mentioned the thrown book.

She nodded. "I wish this were surprising. Thanks for telling me."

"One more thing. It's murky." My body mass was shifting in strange ways. My head felt heavy, then light. I tried to remember what I'd eaten for lunch. "The other day when I was looking for books, I ran into Jeremy and Olivia."

"God, Olivia. You know what's going on in that family?"

"Something with the uncle?"

"I can't talk about it." She rubbed her fingers together in the symbol for money.

Olivia's uncle was defrauding the rest of them? Her mother was a beverage heiress. Cream soda? Something not very glamorous but apparently lucrative.

I said, "That's a relief. I thought it might be—"

"Don't repeat this," she said.

"No."

"It'll be in the papers soon. So Olivia? This can't be good."

"They were in a room together—Jeremy and Olivia. A *Negative Space* meeting? But just the two of them. I was looking for the books, and I didn't open the door right away. They were sitting close together, reading something. They weren't wearing masks."

Robin was silent.

"I was looking to see if the books were there. And he nudged her with his head." *Nuzzled*, I thought.

"Nudged?" She looked like she might smile.

"Leaned into her," I said. "Like you might if you were comforting someone, if you were close."

"OK." She closed her eyes. "That was it?"

"I walked in and Jeremy told me where to find the books."

Robin looked out the window nearest her. It was another clear day, but colder. The air was glassy.

"And?"

"I left."

"You left."

I thought of the meetings in which we were reminded that *we* were adults. It was our duty to wade into discomfort, take charge. The children were in our care. My fingers prickled. *Don't panic*, I told myself.

"What I mean is." Robin bit her lip. "Since you left, maybe you had a sense." She stopped again. "They shouldn't have had the door closed. They shouldn't have been unmasked. The . . . nudge?"

"Nudge."

"We don't know what that was. Have you spoken to Jeremy?"

"No."

"I'll speak to him. I suppose you haven't spoken to Olivia?"

"I wanted to speak to you first."

She gently touched the space between her eyes. "Let's meet again tomorrow. In the morning."

"OK," I said. "Yes. I'm sorry." Jeremy was her friend; they'd worked together for decades.

"Nothing to apologize for." Her voice was wispy.

I took the elevator to the lobby. I needed to get home so Marian could leave, but first I needed to eat. I swept my hand around my bag looking for a protein bar, and thought longingly of the tray of little chocolates that used to be on the security desk. The lights in the lobby shimmered and drifted, like the toys on the surface of Lewis's bath, like the words in the books I read before I slept. The lobby broke into pieces. I woke up looking into the face of Wendy, the school nurse.

IT WAS NOT MY FIRST TIME in the nurse's office. I'd stopped by when I cut my thumb through the nail preparing Jane's fruit in the morning, and another time when I'd had a shock that went up to my shoulder while plugging in the toaster. Both times Wendy, a bony woman with long, elegant hands, who was generally skeptical of pain and discomfort, found me to be in no danger.

"Oh, hello," she said. "You're up."

"I'm sorry," I told her.

"Nothing to apologize for." Robin's words.

"I was hungry."

"Let's get you some orange juice."

"I have to get home for the babysitter."

"You hit your head," she said. "I called Nicholas. He's coming to pick you up."

I started to sit up.

"Put your head between your legs. Your brain needs oxygen." She touched my shoulder.

My head hurt, but I felt relaxed. "Do you think I'm going to die in two days like that actress?"

"You should see your doctor. I don't think you're going to die."

I had an urge to tell Wendy about Jeremy. I wondered if she'd take it as she took everything: without surprise, with only a sliver of interest. But Jeremy was off my plate. The conversation with Robin hadn't gone very well. There was the question of me leaving the room. But I could think of an explanation for that.

I looked over my arms and legs, feeling tenderness for my body. How strange to have lost those—seconds? minutes? How strange, but also, what a nice break. I pictured myself unconscious on the floor, wondered who'd found me, carried me to Wendy. Had Wendy helped carry me? I didn't want to know. I had a rare sense of certainty about this, and the certainty added to my contentment. I *wouldn't* know. If Wendy tried to tell me, I'd stop her. But she didn't try to tell me.

"DRAMA!" NICHOLAS SAID on the walk home. The air was smooth and sunlight fell in yellow strips across the buildings. "What happened?"

"I was really hungry."

"Whatever. On the phone Wendy told me it could be from anxiety."

"What did you say?"

"I said, 'Anxious? That doesn't sound like her.' And we both laughed."

"Fuck you."

"Hang on." He looked at his phone. "I have to take this."

"You're kidding me."

"I had to leave *work*. In the middle of a *meeting*. Look at you, you're fine."

I did feel mostly fine, but my head throbbed. We passed a tree holding a large, shaggy bird's nest, a terrace of thickly packed leaves and branches that looked damp and pliable, as though they'd started to decompose. It wasn't beautiful, but it was probably comfortable, the opposite of Robin's office. I looked down. The sun was too bright.

"I have two comments," Nicholas was saying to the phone. "My first comment . . . No, please, you go first."

"OH, YOU LOOK FINE!" Marian said. The apartment was clean and neat. The books on one of the shelves had been arranged by size. I felt badly for resenting her lowercase *ok*.

Lewis grabbed my legs.

"Lie down!" Jane shouted. "Mom, lie down! Marian says you fainted."

"I'm completely OK. I let myself get too hungry."

"See?" Lewis said. "Mama's not dead."

Yet, I thought, to appease whatever force punishes an excess of confidence.

I ORDERED PIZZA and Lewis and I moved plants so we had a place to eat. Nicholas had been buying houseplants on the internet since he'd recovered from COVID, and most surfaces in our apartment were crowded with cactuses and herbs, as well as more ambitious greenery—a banana plant, a coffee plant. We had slender eucalyptus and olive trees, an umbrella tree that reminded me of my dermatologist's office with its thick, rubbery leaves, a ficus that seemed always on the point of giving up. The plants arrived in soggy cardboard boxes, looking dry and fragile, and shed their leaves alarmingly in the first few days after Nicholas replanted them. But he fussed over them, moving them so some were bathed in afternoon sun while others stayed mostly in shade. He sprayed them with little water bottles, and gently wiped dust from their leaves. He gave them the kind of anxious, dedicated care that he usually reserved for his job, and many of them thrived.

"Papa's gonna be mad," Lewis said, carrying thyme from the kitchen counter to a windowsill. Nicholas didn't like the children to touch the plants.

"This is not the pizza I like," Jane said. "Can you please cut it up?"

"Do you want it cut up, Lewis?" I said.

"No," he said.

I cut Jane's slice into little pieces. It looked messy spread out on the plate.

When I sat down Lewis said, "I do want my pizza cut up."

"Really, Lewis? I think it's better whole," I said.

"I want it cut up," he said.

"I'm not very hungry." Jane pushed her plate away. "I don't like this pizza. But I really appreciate you buying it."

Nicholas took his dinner at his desk in our bedroom, in front of his monitor, which showed a grid of squares, each framing a face. Some of the people were in Hong Kong, where it was very early, some in Australia. Lewis delivered a plate to Nicholas and Jane screamed, "It was my turn, it was my turn. Why does no one in this family think of me? Why, why?"

"Would you like to go get your dad's plate?" I asked her at the end of the meal.

"No," she said. "That's disgusting."

I led Jane and Lewis through their preparations for sleep, squeezing glittery toothpaste onto toothbrushes, looking through the sea of clothes in their drawers for pajamas. While I was helping Lewis into his pajama top, I saw a green bruise in the shape of a heart on his arm. This wasn't unusual. Lewis was often bruised. He'd fallen off every chair and table in our apartment, as well as down stairs and off swings. On days when he didn't fall off something, he still lost his balance, landing on his hands or elbows or face. But I had in my mind meetings with Tonya, and the kinds of bruises that worried people. Worst were symmetrical bruises—

bruises on both upper arms, as though a child had been gripped, shaken—or bruises that looked like fingerprints. I inspected Lewis's other arm as he wriggled, made his body into a ball, hid his arm in the pillowcase.

"Hold still just *one* second," I said. I wasn't concerned that someone might be hurting him, but that the bruise would make it appear that someone was, and that one of his teachers would see it and wonder. But Lewis's other arm wasn't bruised.

I stopped checking Lewis, wishing that I didn't know about the existence of Child Protective Services, and some other things: death, incels, internet chat forums where people compared symptoms and wondered if they had rare and terrible diseases.

"Where did you get this?" I said to Lewis.

"I fell way down."

"Where?"

"On the stairs."

"You fell down the *stairs*?"

"Lewis didn't fall down the stairs," Jane said.

"I did," Lewis said. "Remember in the old apartment yesterday? I fell way down the stairs."

Months ago, in our last apartment building, Lewis had fallen down half a flight of stairs. "I mean where did you get *this* bruise?" I said.

"The stairs," Lewis said.

"Lewis," Jane said. "No—"

Lewis screamed and ran to the bathroom.

"Never mind, Jane," I said.

———

"I WAS SCARED YOU WERE DEAD," Jane said as I lay next to her.

"I'm absolutely not." *Yet.*

"I was so scared."

I felt her toes against my shin. She was already two-thirds my length, would certainly be taller than me.

"Mom?" she said.

"Yes."

"I can't believe humans can be milked like cows, but only babies can do it." She sighed. "I think that's hilarious." She turned toward me. "My mouth hurt today."

"You mean around your teeth? The teeth the dentist talked to us about?"

"I don't know," she said dreamily. "I'll tell you tomorrow."

"Do they still hurt?"

"Do what still hurt?"

"Your teeth."

"My teeth don't hurt."

"You said your mouth hurt."

She rolled away from me. "Never mind." She fell asleep.

I shined the flashlight on my phone onto her cheek, shielding her eyes. Her skin wasn't rosier than usual. I didn't think it was. When she slept, her expression became serious, as though she were concentrating on something; this had been true since she was a baby. I kissed her, nuzzled my face into her hair, which was matted in places; I kept forgetting to brush it.

Nuzzled. But I wouldn't think about that. Anyway, it was out of my hands.

My head hurt in a dull way, and it was sore on the left side, presumably where I'd hit the floor. I saw my body just falling through space. It was the most significant thing—the most significant physical thing—to happen to me since Lewis's birth, and I had missed it; I was only experiencing the aftermath. I turned away from Jane, closed my eyes.

Nicholas had moved from the bedroom to the living room, and I heard him begin a new call.

"They've been working for a year with no cash flow at all? . . . Are you all in different rooms or are you working from home? . . . Different parts of the office . . . So what is the purpose of today's call, exactly? . . . So feedback from the last call we did . . . Is Denise in the room somewhere with you guys? . . . Paul, Denise was going to join, right? Oh, there she is. Fashionably late."

Later, I climbed into bed. Nicholas, connected by his headphones to a phone under his pillow, recoiled from me. "You woke me up. I was *asleep*."

"I fell asleep in Jane's bed," I told him.

"How's your head?"

"It hurts a little."

"I'm not worried about you," he said. "You're tough."

"Do you think so?"

He'd fallen back asleep. I heard the sound of applause coming from his earbuds.

WEDNESDAY

I WOKE UP just before sunrise and brought a glass yogurt jar to the kitchen table with my laptop. We had several of these jars; when the yogurt was finished, I washed them and used them for almonds, coconut flakes, oats. I liked the list of cows' names on the side of the jar. Ethel, Aurelia, Melody, Wilhelmina. I'd looked up the farm on the internet and found pictures of a barn at dusk, a fresh-faced calf, Wilhelmina lying in a big pile of hay. The jar claimed the yogurt was European-style, sour and light tasting. Nicholas said it was all marketing, and he would have been even more critical if he'd known the price; I scratched off the sticker before I put it in the fridge.

Jane and Lewis emerged from their bedroom at the same time, and fought over who would shower first. They took off their clothes, ran to the bathroom, and waited, whining, while the water became warm.

"Let Jane go first," I said, then, "Jane, how about you let Lewis go first?" They ran around me and through the curtain, and struggled, slippery and naked, under the water.

"You must absolutely stop this," I shouted. "This is how people break bones."

"Wait, what do you mean?" Jane said, stepping into a towel. "Like under your skin?"

"Of course under your skin."

"This part?" Jane touched her knee.

"That part, any part, anywhere. Does your mouth hurt?"

"My throat feels scratchy."

"Have a sip of water," I said.

"Does Jane's cheek look red?" I said to Nicholas.

"No." He was holding one phone in each hand. He glanced at Jane. "Maybe a little."

"Really?" I said. "You think it's red?"

"If you're worried, call the doctor."

"Yes," I said. "I just need to get through this meeting with Robin."

"Jane," Nicholas said, "do your teeth hurt?"

"No, but my stomach feels strange. And yesterday my ankle hurt when I went like this." She climbed on the couch and jumped to the floor.

I said to Nicholas, "Can you look at the bumps?"

"What bumps?" he said.

"The bumps over her *teeth*."

"I'm done," Lewis yelled.

I went to the bathroom, holding a towel.

"Show me the bumps," I heard Nicholas tell Jane.

He shouted. Jane was laughing.

"The bumps?" I said.

"No. She has a loose tooth." He shivered. "You know how I feel about those."

———

THE DAY WAS OVERCAST and warm. We took the long way to Lewis's playground to look at the river, gray and opaque like poured cement. "The ducks are gone," Jane said.

At Jane's drop-off, a boy said to Jane's teacher, "It's my mom's birthday today and she got something she's been wanting for over a year."

"Wow," said Jane's teacher. "Mom must be so excited."

"It's a stand mixer," the boy said. "She's making cinnamon rolls right now."

Jane said, "Why don't you make cinnamon rolls?"

"We can make them," I said. "It's a weekend activity. They take time."

"You have time," Jane said. "Your job is only part-time. *Part*-time."

Recently when I'd told her not to make a mess in my bedroom, she'd said, "Actually, it's Dad's bedroom. Dad paid for this whole apartment."

"Your class is lining up," I told Jane, and hugged her. I'd forgotten to brush her hair again.

THE AIR IN THE SCHOOL felt muggy, and in the rig room it was even thicker. Half of the overhead lights weren't working and the room had a shadowy, twilight feeling. There were only a few more weeks of school and the environment was no longer being maintained. The school would become hotter, stuffier, and dimmer until we were released for the summer. I'd heard that some parents touring the school were surprised by the decrepitude of the building. This was a source of pride for the administration—one way in which they were not catering to the clientele. I turned on the air filter and watched the ninth graders traipse in. I was glad to see that Olivia wasn't among them.

We needed to discuss *The Metamorphosis*, but I wasn't prepared for a conversation. My head hurt, and I didn't have any plan about what to say, what not to say. And I was nervous I'd faint, though I'd eaten two scrambled eggs for breakfast. I looked at the lights that were working to be sure they weren't moving in funny ways.

"We'll write today," I said. "At the end of class, you can read, if you'd like." I told them to imagine they had woken up as an animal, to write about their day in a new body.

"Can I write about being an inanimate object?" Luca P. said.

"No," I said. "An animal."

"Can I write about being myself but I don't feel like myself?" said Autumn.

"No," I said.

"How long should it be?" said Sebastian.

"That doesn't matter," I said. "Be specific, use details."

"So it can be very short?"

"You'll need space to fill everything in. Think about how hard it is for Gregor to just get out of bed."

"But that's very human," said Eloise. "That's like a cliché."

Once, in class, Eloise had googled the author of a short story I'd brought in and said, "Wow. I can't believe other people think this stuff is good."

"You know what I mean," I said.

"I know what I'm going to write about," said Daniel, in the room today.

"Rosie can't hear anything," said Eloise. "Look at the chat. You should really be looking at the chat, don't you think?"

Rosie, the only remote student, had written, *I can't hear a thing. I can't hear a thing. I can't hear a thing.*

I said, "Let's test the audio on our end." *Rosie,* I wrote, *we're testing the audio on our end.*

Luca F. went into the hall with his laptop and joined class remotely.

"Can you hear us?" I said.

"Yes," he said, and amazingly his voice was at a reasonable volume.

"Our audio is working *perfectly*," I said.

"That's true," said Daniel, "but Rosie didn't hear you say that." *Our audio is working. Maybe leave and come back?*

"Why don't you just tell her what we're doing in the chat?" said Luca F. "Since we won't be, like, talking?"

"Good idea," I said, but we had to wait for Rosie to come back. When she did, still unable to hear, I described the exercise in the chat.

Can I write about being a plant? Rosie wrote.

An animal, please.

It's OK. I'm going to write about being a salamander. She moved her camera to show an orange creature holding itself very still on the picnic table where she was sitting.

"Oh, I have those at my country house," said Sebastian. "We call them newts."

"Me too," said Aimee. "So many."

"What's the difference between a newt and a salamander?" said Autumn.

Rosie, where are you? Sally wrote in the chat.

Rosie shrugged, smiled.

"Let's get started," I said.

THERE WASN'T TIME FOR the students to read their work, which disappointed no one. "Finish these tonight," I said. "Bring them in tomorrow."

"I'm done," Eloise said. "Can I hand it in now?"

"Give it a once-over tonight," I said.

"It's really done." But she closed her laptop.

Sebastian turned his laptop to show me his screen: a field of white, a few thin paragraphs, amply spaced. "Is this enough?" he said.

"I very much doubt it," I said.

"Where's Olivia?" Daniel said.

"Oh, she never comes to class," Gabriella said.

Luca F. approached my desk. "Do we have to read tomorrow?"

"No," I said. "You don't *have* to." We had this conversation every time the possibility of sharing work came up. Luca F. had a fear of inspiring someone. Earlier in the year, I'd tried to tease it apart. Was he worried about being copied? About not getting credit? No. He said, "I don't like the idea of someone taking something of mine and doing just whatever they want with it." And there was the possibility of a chain of inspiration: his work inspiring another person, whose work would inspire another person, and on and on. It wasn't only reading a story or poem that gave him pause; he was cagey about participating in discussions. It was a paranoid, protective stance, and I was sympathetic.

"You don't *have* to," I said again. "I think you might consider it. You might find inspiring people isn't as bad as you think." I didn't add that the chance of his classmates listening closely enough to be inspired was low.

"But I don't have to?" he said.

"No."

"And you won't show it to anyone? My story?"

"I don't even have your story."

"Tomorrow, after I hand it in."

"I won't," I said, thinking that if it contained any violence, anything that might indicate a troubled state of mind, I would show it to the grade dean and the school psychologist.

"OK," he said. "Thanks. I'm writing about a fox."

"Oh, a fox," I said. "Great choice. Do you know what they eat? I can't wait to read it."

He looked at me with disappointment. I was usually careful to respond with minimal interest to his ideas, so he wouldn't worry he was inspiring me. He was backing away from the desk. "Bye," he said, and left.

"I have a meeting," I called to the back of the room, where Gabriella and Daniel were lingering near a balance beam. "Another class is coming in. Can we please move a little faster?"

THE HALLWAY OUTSIDE ROBIN'S OFFICE was narrow and dark, with a thick carpet. On the walls were a few student self-portraits, and one seemed to look at me, with drowsy eyes and a mildly unpleasing expression. There were low voices and laughter coming from inside, but they stopped when I knocked. Robin opened the door. The sun had come out while I was teaching, and it filled the room, falling evenly on the wooden desk, the paper lamp, and Jeremy, who sat on the church pew, his posture very upright, legs crossed, hands stacked on his knees. He looked energetic, ready to spring up, which he immediately did.

"I'm sure you're surprised to see me! You sit." He opened his arm to the pew.

"Oh no." I thought of sitting on the floor and decided it would be unseemly. "I can sit here." I leaned on the windowsill, felt the sun on my back.

"Are you OK?" Jeremy said.

"We heard you fainted," said Robin.

"I'm completely fine," I said. "I was just hungry."

"Well," said Jeremy, and looked at Robin.

"Well," Robin said, drawing out the word. She was wearing silver earrings shaped like tiny eggs. She touched one and tilted her head, as though she were listening to it. "We think." She looked at Jeremy. "This may be a misunderstanding." She spoke deliberately, giving emphasis to *misunderstanding*.

"You must be upset," Jeremy said. "I know how conscientious you are."

I looked between them, grateful for the cover of my mask.

"Why don't you explain?" Robin said to Jeremy.

"I wasn't wearing a mask." He touched his blue surgical mask. "We had the door closed. Olivia must have closed it. No wonder you were suspicious."

"Not suspicious," I said.

"Not suspicious. No wonder you were *concerned* when you thought you saw me touch her. With my head. But I didn't. I didn't nudge her." He looked like he might be smiling when he said *nudge*.

Nuzzle, I thought. "Oh?"

"It was the angle. I reached across her—I remember this—to pick up a pencil. We were discussing her contribution to *Negative Space*. It covered delicate material. Well, Olivia. What do you think she wrote about?" He looked at Robin. "It's *thinly* veiled."

She brought her gaze to the ceiling. "It'll be in the *Post* tomorrow. We'll all be relieved."

"The cleansing power of sunlight," Jeremy said.

"Having it hush-hush is making everyone crazy. Not least Olivia."

"The stuff with her uncle?" I said.

Robin zipped her fingers across her mask, sealing her lips.

"How is Erin dealing with it?" Jeremy said. Erin was Olivia's sister, a senior at the school.

Robin shrugged. "Not a peep. Everything rolls off that one."

Jeremy turned to me. "I'm sure my face looked troubled. I *am* troubled by this whole *situation*."

"It's depressing when people are so—" Robin stopped. "Just exactly the way they are." She gave a huff.

"Greedy?" I said.

Jeremy raised his eyebrows. "It is certainly unoriginal," he said. "The point is, when I reached across to get the paper, you thought my head nudged hers." The smile again. "Because of the angle. You told Robin it looked like I was comforting her. I wish someone could give that child some comfort."

"It's so sad," said Robin absently, looking at something on her computer, which had been chirping and babbling as emails, texts, and reminders came in. She shook her head, pulled her eyes from the screen. "Her mother and I went to college together."

"Valerie," Jeremy said. "Until recently she was making beer. Very good beer, actually."

They traded facts about Valerie, whose beer was served at high-end restaurants all over the city.

"I don't like beer," I said. "I've never had a beer I'd call delicious."

Robin said, "I *do* like beer, but this was something else entirely."

"I guess beverages are in her blood," Jeremy said.

I said, "Is the money from cream soda? Is that right?"

Jeremy said, "I think she was happy to shut it down when

COVID started. I don't think she expected it to take off the way it did. And she never liked working."

"I met her brother once," Robin said. "He had a funny way of breathing, like he was panting. And I heard when he was younger." She stopped and looked at me, maybe remembering she needed to be careful about what she said, or maybe she wanted me to ask another question about Olivia's uncle, so that she could again tell me she wasn't at liberty, had said too much. *Don't repeat this.*

Jeremy looked at his watch and stood up. "I have a class."

"Do you have a second?" Robin said to me.

Jeremy said, "You two should speak." He looked at me. "I'm sorry. It must have been distressing."

When he was gone Robin said, "I want to make sure you're OK. I want to make sure this makes sense to you."

"It does," I said. "I understand what Jeremy is saying." Jeremy had come up with an explanation, what I'd been hoping for. If I agreed to it, the matter would be officially closed. But it wouldn't really be off my plate. I said, "I did see their heads touch."

A FEW MONTHS AGO, napkins and food scraps had started to appear every few days on the fire escape of my apartment—bread crusts in tissuey paper, an apple core, ribbons of lettuce.

The first time it happened, Nicholas accused me.

"What have you been doing out here?" he said, pointing to a waxed muffin wrapper, opened like a flower over the metal slats.

"You aren't serious," I said.

"I'm half serious."

"It's obviously the raccoon." A raccoon sometimes came to the window boxes, observing us intently for a few moments. "Or a squirrel."

"Or a rat." Nicholas liked to upset me with the possibility of a rat. We'd once had a mouse problem; he called them rats.

"It's not a rat."

I entertained the idea that it was me, that I'd experienced some kind of *episode* and eaten a sandwich on our fire escape. People raided their pantry under the influence of sleeping pills, and I took valerian at night. Or maybe Nicholas, who often seemed on the brink of a breakdown due to his job, had finally completely lost his mind. Soon enough, we saw a squirrel frantically chewing a heel of baguette inches from the window. Since this happened, I'd decided to be more empirical in my judgments, to trust my memory.

I hadn't seen Jeremy's head move *past* Olivia's head; I'd seen it move *into* Olivia's head. Gently. I didn't want to believe that it had gone further than this, but he'd nudged or nuzzled her. I had seen it. And I couldn't be sure it had stopped there. I regretted not knowing Olivia better, so that I could say with more certainty what she might and might not do, how she would and wouldn't act in different circumstances. I regretted not being the kind of person who could make these judgments in the absence of exhaustive knowledge.

"You're sure this is what you saw?" Robin said.

I said, "It's what I saw."

"OK." Robin put her head in her hands. I was disappointing her, which was not unpleasurable. It was probably how members of the administration felt when they shrugged their shoulders in the face of parents complaining about the school building. I usually bent my will to Robin's—it was hardly a decision—and not bending my will was a loosening, like removing an earring I'd forgotten I was wearing.

"I'll have to speak to Jeremy again," Robin said.

I said, "I wonder if someone should speak to Olivia?"

"That would be a good idea," said Robin. "There is the question of how to approach it now that we have a—discrepancy."

"Yes."

"Let me think about this. Let's loop in Tonya."

"OK."

"I'll talk to her," Robin said. "You probably should, too."

I LEFT ROBIN'S OFFICE for the steps outside, still cool, though the sun was strong. The sun warmed my clothes and my skin, and soon I was completely warm; my nerves were quiet. It was good to be in the fresh air, a brick wall between me and everyone in the school. It allowed me to think. Now, in addition to the nudge or nuzzle, there was Jeremy's lie, vivid and distinct, a fact. Lies were always a surprise, in spite of evidence that most people lied continuously and reflexively. The students lied, my children lied, Nicholas lied. I lied in the narratives I wrote about my students, but those weren't *wholesale* fabrications; they were just editing, spiffing up. They were not, in any event, sinister. I didn't think they were.

I knew Jeremy was lying, and of course Jeremy knew, but Robin didn't seem to know, or didn't want to know. Again I returned to the question of what the lie was about: a nudge or a nuzzle, the beginning of something, or a sign of something underway, or an off moment, one he'd decided it was best to pretend never happened. Darya was heading in and stopped to say hello to me.

"Done for the day?"

I shook my head. "Just taking a breather."

"Do you know—hang on."

"Who?" Olivia, I thought. It occurred to me, for the first time, that Darya might also be receiving *my* emails.

"Ivan," she said.

"Oh," I said. "No." Of course there was nothing in my email about Olivia.

"His parents took him off his medication again," she said.

"And that's bad?"

"I'm not meant to talk about this."

"I won't say anything."

She sat down, adjusting a strap on her overalls, which were canvas, cream colored, and did not, like some overalls, make her look like a child. She was carrying a large bag, which she put between her feet; a few branches of eucalyptus escaped from one side.

ahead and the other dentist was waiting for us. "He's excellent," Jane's dentist said. "I wish he'd been in practice when my children were young." Dentistry had changed over the last decade, and the dentists I interacted with were reassuring, kind, even solicitous. They were still extremely expensive.

"You are not going to die," I said to Jane. *Yet*, I thought, and immediately, *No, never, never.*

"Is it going to hurt?" she said.

"You won't feel it," I said. "It might hurt a bit afterward. It sometimes does. You get to have ice cream for dinner."

"I don't want it to hurt. Oh, I'm so scared."

"It's normal to be scared." I was trying to avoid glancing at her cheek, which looked warm and inflamed. "It's a new experience. But it isn't dangerous. Does it hurt now?"

"A little," Jane said.

"The point is to make it hurt less."

"But will it hurt?"

"Also," I said, "you can tell Lewis all about it."

"I wish I was Lewis," Jane wailed. "I'm so scared I can't stand it."

"You can be scared," I said, "but you can't drag like this. We'll never get there."

"I don't *want* to get there." I saw Jane move through a psychic door into panic. She collapsed, hung her body weight from my arm, brought us to a stop. I made my arm loose, unwound my hand from hers, and continued walking, leaving her in a pile on the sidewalk. There was a damp-looking spot close to where she'd landed. Spilled water, I thought, optimistically.

"We have to get there," I called, looking over my shoulder. "The doctor needs to get rid of the bumps."

She stood and ran to me, hobbling and half doubled over with fear. "I don't want to get rid of the bumps," she said. "I like the bumps. Don't let him take them. Oh why, why, why?"

THE DENTIST'S OFFICE HAD panoramic views. On one side were rooftops, which rippled through Manhattan, and on the other the river, shimmering and dotted with little boats. The buildings from this height looked graceful and insubstantial, and even less real than they did from the top floors of the school. The view would soon be blocked by a tower going up next door, but this wasn't a problem, said Shannon, who sat at the front desk, because they were moving to the new building once it was completed. Shannon smelled like mint chewing gum. In front of her desk lay a retriever with shining fur, and Jane threw herself on top of the animal, putting her face into his neck. Our dog had died the year before.

Shannon came out from behind the desk. She was wearing a pleated skirt that expanded and contracted like a jellyfish when she moved. "That's Leo," she said to Jane, crouching and touching the dog's nose. "He's an old man."

She asked if Jane would like to pick out toys for after the procedure, and led her to a wooden chest in the corner of the room, where Jane found a velvet bag of gemstones and a thumb-sized action figure. Holding these carefully and a little in front of her, as though they were amulets that might offer protection, she followed Shannon through a hallway and around a corner to the procedure room. Shannon helped Jane into the chair and took the stones and figure from her, complimenting Jane on her good taste and saying she would look after them. "You're going to take a tiny nap," she said.

"I'm not tired," Jane said, looking around Shannon to me.

"It's a special kind of nap. You don't have to be tired."

Shannon moved calmly, and her hands where they touched Jane were gentle. She pinned green paper over Jane's chest and patted her arm, as though she were tucking her into bed. Her fingernails were short and lemon yellow. "She's so beautiful," Jane whispered to me.

"This will be simple." The dentist had a low voice and the cheerful demeanor of the floaters at Lewis's school. "I'd like to remove both teeth," he said. "We have to sedate her, anyway. The other side looks fine, but this way you won't have to think about it."

These people made problems disappear. They did it as if it were nothing. The dentist fitted a plastic mask over Jane's mouth and nose and counted down from ten while she drifted into unconsciousness. Another woman had materialized, wearing a paper coat and glasses to shield her eyes. She put a hand on my shoulder. "I'm Laurie," she whispered. "I help during the procedures." She brought me to the waiting room.

I sat on a chair near Leo, who shifted his body to put his head over my feet. There was a low hum from a noise machine in the room, and I began to think of the sounds being muffled, the things happening in Jane's mouth. Shannon was telling me about the new office. They'd gotten a deal: "Nothing to it." She'd learned how to negotiate from her parents, who had a business importing specialty foods—tinned fish, olives. There would be floor-to-ceiling windows, more light, a more generous view.

"I'm only worried about him," she said, looking at Leo. "He doesn't like change."

"Is he yours?" I asked.

"He's Patrick's. I take him when he gives talks and things." The dentist traveled to dental schools and conferences around the country. He was a celebrity in the world of pediatric dentistry. I had a moment of gratitude for Nicholas's job, which came with dental benefits for all of us. "That was before COVID," Shannon went on. "Now I just take him when I know I need a dog around. You know that feeling?"

"Our dog died last year," I said.

"You do know, then."

I thought about working at the dentist's office, spending the day in the light-filled rooms, taking Leo for walks and learning from Shannon how to navigate the real estate market. How to soothe children. I wondered what she ate for breakfast, what time she went to sleep at night, but my interest only revealed the gulf between us. Shannon wouldn't imitate the habits of another person.

There were websites wholly given to minutiae, the practices of the famous and unfamous—whether they drank coffee or tea, how they exercised, their favorite brands of underwear. I'd spent evenings, as Jane fell asleep, scanning interviews on my phone,

learning about the little routines of chefs, herbalists, social work-
ers. It was mostly opaque and unrevealing, often boring. Reading
the interviews could feel like folding laundry, working my way
through a heap of clothes. It could make me think I was wasting
my life. "Of course it's inane," my friend Jessica said. "Who cares
what strangers eat for lunch." Nicholas said, "The surprise is not
that it's dull; it's that you expected otherwise." And Irene, from
school, whom I'd also spoken to about it, said, "The only point of
those interviews is to make you buy the underwear."

But I wanted to know. If I could fit myself into the pattern
of Shannon's behaviors, maybe I'd gradually become a more nim-
ble, pragmatic person, the kind of person who dealt with a disap-
pearing view by acquiring a new and better view. If Shannon had
been in the midst of the Jeremy situation, she wouldn't have gotten
caught up in parsing whether she'd seen a nudge or a nuzzle.

I'd start by asking Shannon, "Are you a breakfast person?" Then
I'd explain the scene between Jeremy and Olivia, and the conversation with Robin and Jeremy. I *should* start with Jeremy, but I might
never get back to breakfast, and I'd long thought if I could find the
right thing to eat in the morning, the entire day would improve.
In the end there wasn't time for any of it, because Laurie fetched
me to retrieve Jane.

Jane woke from the procedure groggy and puffy, but clean.
(*There was some blood on your cheek*, my mother would say. *You
were so unsteady on your feet.*) I waved goodbye to Shannon and
patted Leo, but Jane didn't seem to register either of them as we
left the office.

"CLOSE THE DOOR SOFTLY," the taxi driver said. "It's an old car."

I pulled the door closed.

"You think that's soft?" he said. "Good thing I said something."

The divider between the front and back seats was papered with advertisements for a supplement to improve energy, longevity, metabolism, and sleep.

"I was in a purple tornado," Jane said. "I *almost* fell over. Someone was telling me to blow up a balloon. Don't you think the dentist is so kind? Can I go back next week? What was the woman's name?"

"You mean Shannon or the other woman?"

"There were two women?" Jane put her head against the window. "The one who gave me toys. She had great style. Do you have my jewels? What other woman?"

"Does it hurt?" I asked.

"I'm tired," she said. "I can't talk about it now."

As Jane dozed, the driver told me about his previous car, a green sedan, destroyed in a side-impact collision in the nineties. The car had to be sawed open to extract his passenger, who was taken away in an ambulance. The driver in the other car had run a red light. He fled the scene on foot, and when his car was searched, he was found to have fake insurance.

"The worst moment of my life," the driver said. "I don't know what happened to my passenger. My friends said don't follow it, don't find out." He'd stopped driving for a long time, and had only recently resumed. "I drove people to the hospital," he said. "I don't know what happened to them either."

"But you never got sick?" I said.

He shook his head. "I was careful about the mask."

He continued to be careful. His body was already in a state of dysregulation, from his poor diet as a young man, as well as the unrelenting adjustments of daylight savings. He was worried about the effects of the vaccine, but in the end he took it, persuaded by his niece, a doctor. He'd done a little research, though, and believed he'd received the shot with the least amount of filler. "I'm an unusual patient," he concluded. "This is the only vaccine I've ever gotten."

"I've had them all," I said. "I think—" But I didn't want to start doling out medical advice, and he was also silent, perhaps feeling something similar. We continued slowly home. He stopped for yellow lights, some green lights that he seemed to suspect were about to change.

"He's tired," he said. People often called Jane *he* because of her short hair. She had fallen asleep.

"We were just at the dentist. They gave her gas."

"I have to get to the dentist." He touched his jaw. "Next month. Maybe the month after that. It's too much money." He laughed.

"No," Jane said as I pulled her from the car. "Let me rest! Let me rest!"

"You can rest all afternoon," I said. "But not here. We have to get upstairs."

"No," Jane said. "Oh I hate you." But she let me drag her from the taxi.

"Careful!" the driver said as I went to close the door. "Softly, softly."

LEWIS AND I ROASTED MUSHROOMS for dinner. I pulled off stems and he dipped the tops in oil and spread them on a sheet pan, placing them first in a circle, then huddled around the edge, then in orderly rows. He ate half of them right when they came out of the oven, and refused the ones I put on his plate, with rice and scrambled eggs. Nicholas ate dinner with us.

"Did you make this, Lewis?" he said.

"No," Lewis said.

"You did," I said. "You helped."

"Just the mushrooms," Lewis said dismissively. "You know what's funny?" He pronounced his *f*s as *h*'s. A *farm* was a *harm*. *Funny* was *hunny*.

"What's funny?" I said.

"Jane is sleeping."

Jane was on the couch, eyes closed, her face inches away from a tablet playing the otter show.

Nicholas put dishes in the sink and I rubbed Jane's head and woke her. "Jane," I said. "You can go right back to sleep, but first you have to rinse your mouth with salt water."

"*What?*" she said. "No. The bumps are gone."

"The bumps are gone," I said, "but there's still just a chance of infection, so we need to keep the spots clean. Just for the week."

"What was the *point?*"

She followed me to the sink and shrieked after the first sip of salt. "It hurts, it hurts."

I helped her change into pajamas, and let Lewis pick any clothes he wanted to wear to bed. He chose shorts and a shirt of Jane's that reached his knees. When they were both in their beds, Jane whispered, "Lewis, I know how to spell *die*."

"I think rice is good for my body," Lewis said as he was falling asleep.

I CHECKED MY EMAIL FROM Lewis's bed. Jeremy wanted to know how Jane was doing. I wrote, *She's fine. I think she'll go to school tomorrow.* And there was an email intended for Darya from a grade dean. *Sorry for the delay. Glad to discuss. Share your concerns.* I thought, *Ivan.* Tonya had also written: *I hear we should talk. Tomorrow?*

My eyes were dry, and my head was starting to hurt again. The pain came and went. I'd go to urgent care. There was a nice doctor there, older and very kind. Once I'd taken Lewis to him and he'd prescribed a cough syrup, calling it an *elixir*. "He's like Mary Poppins," I told Jane, who said, "But he's a *man*." I took out my contacts and put them in the pocket of my sweatpants.

I thought of moving to my own bed, but Nicholas was talking to his family on Zoom and I didn't want to be asked to join. His father was going on about Norwich terriers. "One in five is a good dog, one in ten is a great dog." Years ago I'd taken care of a Norwich terrier puppy for Nicholas's sister when she was out of town.

The dog peed all over the apartment and ate every piece of garbage we passed on the street. I strongly disliked that terrier, and when I brought her on walks I worried that people would notice and ascribe to me an inner coldness, a deep failure of compassion. Then I'd adopted my own dog, not a Norwich terrier, and discovered I was capable of bonding with a puppy. I turned to face Lewis and let the sound of his breathing put me to sleep.

THURSDAY

I WOKE UP and the city was covered in blue shadows, as though it were underwater. I brought my laptop to the soft rag rug Lewis had thrown up on two weeks ago. He'd been in my arms while I was on the phone with Nicholas saying Lewis was fine—he hadn't eaten breakfast—when he threw up all over me, himself, the rug. I'd taken off Lewis's clothes and brought him to the shower, with a plastic bowl and spoon to play with, and a dry towel nearby so he could wipe water from his face. Jane had hung around me, saying, "Am I sick, too? Am I going to throw up?"

Lewis had a delicate stomach; he threw up often, and each time the fallout amazed me—the amount of laundry, the difficulty of eliminating the smell. No school, the babysitter wouldn't come—nobody wanted to be near a sick kid. And the fear that what was happening was worse than it appeared, that I wasn't seeing a stomach virus but a deceptively familiar early symptom of something that in its full expression would be strange and terrible. In the first moments of my children's illnesses, whatever illness, I denied anything was happening. *Jane isn't very hot*, I would tell myself. *She feels warm because she's been running around. Lewis's voice isn't really scratchy, and because of climate change, allergies last through all four seasons.*

I picked at one of the loose strands on the rug, long and dark and curved like a snake. When I walked between the bedroom and the bathroom at night, I avoided the strand. The rug came from a vintage furniture store and I liked to bring to mind the people who'd walked on it, tugged its edges straight, vacuumed it clean. Jane, with her obsession, thought only of dead people's feet, and wouldn't walk on the rug at all.

"We don't *know* the former owner is dead." I didn't mention all the things around us, including other rugs, that were older than the rag rug and had definitely been touched and cared for by people now dead.

I folded the end of the rug so the frayed part was hidden underneath. A good doctor had told me to think of myself as a custodian of my body with its genetic quirks, and of my mind with its neuroses. I was a custodian of other things, too—of some rugs and a dresser, of a silver ring that looked like a snail, of Lewis and Jane. It was an agreeably simple way to see things; it seemed to show the way forward: clean the children, feed them vegetables, wash the rug.

Jane came out of the bedroom and I scrutinized her face, which looked strange, its arrangement slightly shifted. But the swelling seemed better.

"How do you feel?" I asked.

"I'm tired." She lay on the couch.

I said, "Just let me know when you're ready to get in the shower. Or maybe Lewis should take the first shower today."

I made French toast, soaking the bread in the egg and milk for a long time so that even the crust was soft. I let Lewis help, gave him a square of butter to drop into the pan.

"I know you don't want to do this part," I said, turning a slice of bread in the egg. "You don't like to get your hands messy."

"I don't like to wash my hands," he said.

I had to make a piece for Nicholas, too, out of politeness, but I didn't enjoy preparing breakfast for him, as though I'd slipped into the grooves of *housewife, stay-at-home-mom.* "Here you go," I said.

"Oh, thank you," he said. "What a treat."

"But next time you can make your own breakfast."

He stared at me for a moment and took his plate into the bedroom.

"Mom," Jane said, "I don't think you should be so rude to Dad."

"Papa makes the best French toast," Lewis said. He came over to me. "I love you," he said, in a throwaway tone, and kissed my knee.

THE AIR WAS WARM AND DAMP, and everyone on the street had a sheen to their skin. "I'm too tired to walk," Lewis said, and sat cross-legged on the sidewalk, but he couldn't stick with it the way Jane could. "Get up, Lewis," I said, and he did.

At his drop-off, one of the floaters, a woman with floral tattoos along her arm, stopped me and said, "He's been playing with Alice."

"Playing with someone?"

"Playing near her."

I looked around, trying to remember which one was *Alice.* The little girl who wore party dresses to school? The tiny one whose mask covered most of her face?

"Alice, you know." The floater gestured to a small stone-faced child in a gray dress, gray tights, shiny Mary Janes.

"Give me your phone," the girl said smoothly to her father. "I want to do the health check."

When we were definitely on the way to her school, I began to worry about Jane. I said, "If it starts to hurt, if you need to come home, you know you can, right?"

"No," Jane said. "I thought you wouldn't let me come home." She pulled at her sleeves. "It's much too hot. Can I take off my shirt?"

"It isn't that hot."

"I've seen men with their shirts off. Grown-up men." She looked around, trying to find one.

"I don't think anyone is allowed to go to school without a shirt."

"I don't want to go to school. My *teeth*."

"You don't have to go to school," I said. "We do know that if you don't go in today, it'll be harder tomorrow."

"OK."

Her acquiescence worried me more. We walked quietly for another block, Jane skipping or jogging every few steps to keep up. "There's one!" she said.

"One what?"

"Look."

Half a block ahead of us, Olivia and her sister were walking side by side. They must have turned onto the street while I'd been considering Jane's cheeks.

"Not there," Jane said. "There."

Olivia brushed against Erin and Erin moved easily away from

her and back in. They were small and from this vantage point looked not much older than Jane, and just like regular children; you couldn't tell that they were in the midst of a family scandal, that people were talking—speculating—about them.

"*There*," Jane said.

On the other side of the street was a man in running shorts and no shirt. The skin on his back was thick and pale, slippery with sweat. "He's just exercising," I said, and turned back to Olivia and Erin. Where were they headed so early in the morning? Not to school, which was in the other direction. We were going to reach them and pass them. I held Jane back.

"What are you doing?" she said.

"I'm tired this morning. Slow down."

Olivia walked into Erin again and this time Erin gave her a shove. Olivia tripped and moved back to Erin, put her head on Erin's shoulder.

When Jane was an infant, I used to hear the argument that you should have a second child to provide your first with a friend. I was an only child, so this was insulting—the implication that my life was lacking. And the idea of creating a friend—for a *baby*—was creepy, as though the second child were an elaborate doll. But when Jane asked me, "Why *did* you have Lewis?" it wasn't as though I had a good answer.

And when I was young and into adulthood, I'd fantasized about an ideal sibling, intelligent and funny, with common sense, but not so much that she became dull. She would be different from me in critical ways so that I didn't suffer from the comparison. I imagined her bringing me little gifts and passing along her clothing, accompanying me to the doctor, handing me a Klonopin when I ran out. She would know exactly how to read the situation between Jeremy and Olivia, and what to do about it.

"Stop staring, Mom," Jane said.

"Shhhh," I said, but they didn't look back.

They turned at the next block, Erin taking Olivia's wrist and dragging her around the corner. They were saying something to each other now, and Olivia brought her hand to her face. I couldn't tell if she was smiling or frowning.

"Who are those girls?" Jane said. "You're obsessed with them."

"Don't say that." But *obsessed* was just one of her words. Usually she was the object of obsession. Lewis was obsessed with Jane, my mother was obsessed with her, I was obsessed with her. Once, after cuddling a stranger's dog on the street—a dog she'd asked the owner to pet—Jane had turned to me and said, "Oh my god, that dog was obsessed with me."

"One of them is a student of mine," I told her.

"She looked like a grown-up," Jane said.

"I thought she looked young."

"The one with black hair looked young," Jane said.

"That's my student."

"The other one looked as old as the hills."

JANE'S TEACHER WAS LEANING against the fence, smiling in a way that was friendly and somewhat absent. I believed this expression was just for the parents; I had seen glimpses of warmer, more familiar looks directed to Jane and her classmates. I trusted this teacher, even though I didn't really know her. We shared a belief that parents didn't need to be very involved with their children's homework, and I had the impression that she loved Jane. ("All that parents want to feel is that you love their child," Irene had once said.) Jane had announced one night that her teacher ran marathons, didn't own a television, and grew all the herbs she cooked with on her fire escape.

"We grow some herbs, too," I said. "Did you tell her that?"

"Hers are doing much better," Jane said. "I've seen pictures."

"Jane's mouth is still sore," I told the teacher now. "I can always come get her. Or Marian can." If Jane just made it through the first couple of hours, it *would* be Marian to pick her up.

"We'll take care of her." She put her arm around Jane. "She can take it easy today."

I WALKED TO SCHOOL. Now I was expecting to see Olivia, but I didn't, though the neighborhood swarmed with teachers and students, administrative and building staff, and I could pick them out easily, even from a distance, even when I barely knew them. A pair of black shoes, or the slope of a person's shoulders, or something I couldn't begin to identify but that my brain had registered and stored away, would make me think, *Oh, that's the Tuesday–Thursday librarian, that's the new math teacher, that's the child who sits across from the elevators on the third floor.* I was sometimes ashamed of this—recognizing people who likely wouldn't recognize me. It seemed to suggest I was too interested in the lives of strangers. But Nicholas had told me he could also recognize people from far away and assumed it was a universal ability, probably an evolutionary holdover from a time when losing your group could mean quick starvation.

I'd just sat on the steps in front of the school to text Marian when Jeremy walked out of the building. "I was looking for you," he said. "Walk around the block?" We'd taken this walk a few times, including just after I'd interviewed for the job. *I enjoy walking in circles*, he'd said.

"Sure," I said.

He pointed to my bags. "You want to leave those inside?"

"No," I said. "I hear it's good for your bones to carry heavy things."

He looked at me for a moment. "OK."

We turned the corner, to a wide, tree-lined street. People put their babies to sleep here, and there were some mothers and babysitters out now, most of them looking at something on a phone.

"You've had a difficult week," Jeremy said. "Is Jane alright?"

"I think so," I said. "Just bruised."

"And you? Did you hit your head?"

I touched the back of my head, looking for the tender spot.

"I'm sure you'll be fine. I fainted once. I landed on concrete. My head hurt for a couple of weeks, that was it."

"Where did you faint?" I said. "Do you know why?"

"Panic attack," Jeremy said. "It's rare to faint from one. Did I tell you I used to get panic attacks?"

"No. I didn't know that."

"In my twenties and then never again."

"Well, that's good. That they stopped. That your head was OK." Panic attacks, fainting, arrhythmias—things piled up as you got older. I had my own pile, not as big as Jeremy's. Yet.

We turned the corner.

"I hope we keep this stuff after COVID," Jeremy said, gesturing to some tables on the street in front of a pizza place. They'd put up a little white fence, with a vine of pink and blue plastic flowers looped over it.

"It's pretty, but I've heard it attracts rats."

"That's true," he said. "A rat ran by my table the other night."

"Once I stepped in a rat."

"What?"

"I stepped in a rat that had been run over by a car. Fortunately, I was on my way to therapy."

I stopped talking. Not reciprocating friendliness was an act of will, but it made me feel dramatic and artificial. I tried not to look at Jeremy. We turned another corner. A couple of students were lingering at the crosswalk, and one of them, a tall boy, handsome, whose face was covered in acne, smiled at Jeremy, who looked at his watch.

"Where should you be right now?" he said to the boy.

"Oh, I'm heading back in a few," the boy said, and when Jeremy stopped and looked at him, "Really. I won't be late."

We kept walking.

"Has Nicholas started traveling again?" Jeremy said.

"Soon he will."

"Must be hard on you. The two kids, this place. Overwhelming even to think about it."

I often felt harassed, as though I'd stubbed the same toe repeatedly over the course of the day. During the weekend, I'd carry a book with me from room to room, from the couch to the table, from the table to the couch, starting and restarting the same sentence. Sometimes it seemed that all my family did was insult one other and complain. "If you hadn't had Lewis," Jane had said recently, through tears, "I would have had a peaceful life. *A peaceful life.*" Sometimes, when my children were sleeping, or walking into their schools, I would feel a drowning kind of love, mixed with guilt and a sense of loss piling upon loss and more losses to come. And very occasionally, for a moment or two, it would be as though I was lying on a warm dock, listening to water pleat itself in little waves; my mind would be clear; I would feel content.

What Jeremy said—*overwhelming*—barely touched it. Before, I might have explained to him about seeing myself as a *custodian.* I felt the weight of my bags and quickened my pace. "I have to get back," I said. He put a hand on my arm.

"You were right to speak to Robin. You handled the whole thing perfectly. I mean that."

"Thank you."

"The mask, the door. I forget the new rules. Things were so different even a few years ago."

"I've been thinking about that."

"*I* was just thinking"—he stopped walking and looked at me closely—"after I left Robin's office, I was thinking that as I reached past Olivia, I could have bumped into her. With my head, I mean. You might have seen a bump—maybe, I don't remember—but not a nudge. The point is you weren't *seeing* things."

"Oh," I said. "That would explain it."

"I bend the rules. I can't take certain rules seriously."

"I know." We'd talked about new rules around office behavior and how inhuman they were, how we'd turned over moral considerations to consultants who seemed to be emissaries from some giant, corporate HR department: they were cold, defensive, always had an eye on litigation.

"But I'd never—" Jeremy left what he'd never do unsaid.

I didn't want to say anything. If it had been a bump, that would really close the matter. Jeremy and even Robin seemed very interested in closing it, and I was in the unfamiliar position of not being sure I could *let* them. Jeremy scratched his face. His cheeks were almost gaunt, but he didn't look fragile. Some people aged this way, becoming thinner, ropier, scraped down to what was essential.

"I'm turning *Negative Space* over to Charlie," Jeremy said. "Olivia has become too comfortable. I'm not suited for these confidences."

We turned the final corner and were back on the block of the school. Parents were waiting at the door, and some of them, surely, were important people, serious people, people I would be too frightened to speak to under most circumstances. But they were preening, reminding me of the teenagers on the church steps, and as a group they looked silly and undignified.

"I don't think Charlie is suited for any confidences," I said.

"She'd never make them to Charlie." He smiled and held my eyes for a moment, and I thought, *Is he boasting?*

A man detached himself from the parent group and came over to us. "I had to say hello."

Jeremy smiled and put out his hand. "You? You're here?"

The man pulled Jeremy into an embrace and they stood like that briefly before they separated, still grinning at each other. I thought of Jeremy's soft voice, all his little habits. He was like an *invitingly worn* cabinet, one you'd run your hands over without thinking about it.

"I'm heading in," I said.

He turned to me, as though he'd forgotten I was there. "We're almost done, we've almost made it," he said, shaking his fist in a gesture of solidarity.

I WENT TO 503 to look for the *Midsummer*s. If the books weren't there, I'd give the sixth grade a Goethe maxim and ask them to write something inspired by it. Earlier in the year I'd done this with the ninth grade, and when I got to the word *inspired*, I gave Luca F. a look, which he returned without comprehension.

503 was a small room, hardly bigger than a closet, used for student-teacher meetings. It had a square table and a small screened window, and its walls were lined with novels and plays teachers

didn't want to carry to the book room in the sub-sub-basement. The window in the door was covered with a sheet of paper and had been for months. I assumed someone had put it up during the last lockdown drill and forgotten to remove it.

I knocked briefly, opened the door, and found myself standing between Charlie and a woman I recognized, the mother of one of my former sixth graders. They were both sitting at the table, and they weren't wearing masks.

"Sorry," I said. "I was looking for *Midsummers*."

"Come on in," Charlie said, greeting me with more enthusiasm than usual. I didn't feel like I was interrupting, and if I was, it was completely fine.

She was thin and tall, with a bird face. ("You can either have a bird face, a horse face, or a pudding face," a friend once told me, seriously. "You and I have bird faces, which is the middle. The best is a pudding face; the worst, of course, is a horse face.") She wore a black dress made of delicate, filmy fabric, draped and folded in complicated ways.

She was smiling, and stood and said, "I saw *Midsummers*. I remember you, don't I?"

"I taught Elodie last year."

"I'm sorry. They keep us so separate, almost as if they don't trust us together!" She looked at Charlie, who exclaimed, "Ha!"

"We're old friends," he said.

"There they are." Elodie's mother pointed to the top shelf. "I can reach them."

I liked Elodie's mother, and Elodie. She'd given me a begonia in a clay pot before the winter break. I hated Elodie's father, who had regarded me coolly during her conference and said, "She's always been more *enthusiastic* about English. I wonder what we can do about that?"

"I hear you're taking over *Negative Space*," I said.

"Don't remind me," Charlie said. "The last time, I told myself, never again. I told Jeremy, never again. Things have a way of coming back around." He looked to Elodie's mother, who said, "Oh, stop."

"There's hardly anything left to do," he continued. "Just harass the printer so we receive it before the end of the year. Do you remember what happened two years ago? When Tim was running it? Were you here then?"

The printer had gone bankrupt and it hadn't come out until September. You couldn't mention it around Tim.

"I don't care if it's late," Charlie said. "I won't lose any sleep. These kids rarely deal with frustration."

So Jeremy was right; no teenager would tell Charlie her secrets.

"This year has been plenty frustrating," Elodie's mother said.

"I have a student attending class from Colorado, when he isn't on a chairlift. I thought he'd come more when the snow melted, but he has a kayak."

"Sounds like a nice year for him," I said. "But there are other—"

Charlie said, "I'm not being *critical*. I'd love to be in Colorado."

Elodie's mother said, "*Negative Space* is lucky to have you." She'd made neat piles of *Midsummer*s on the table. I put as many as would fit into my bag, and made a stack of the others to carry.

"I'm so glad to see you," she said. "To put a face to a name—

again. Elodie has him this year." She looked at Charlie. "She said last year's teacher—that's you!—was much nicer. She's usually scared of teachers, and she wasn't scared of you at all."

This revealed just what was wrong with my teaching, and Charlie met my eyes with a wry smile, but I was sure she'd meant it as a compliment. Kindness was like a reflex for her, you could sense that, but it didn't seem meaningless. If I'd had more time, I'd have found a way to ask her what she ate for breakfast, how she wound down at the end of the day.

"Tell her *happy reading*," I said, and immediately regretted it. "Tell her have a good summer."

She smiled. "I will."

"Happy reading to you!" Charlie said as I left.

I WALKED TO MY CLASS, fizzy and untethered, but the dense air of the rig room realigned things. My eyes adjusted to the low light, and the stuffiness was like a towel, stamping out all remaining flickers of adrenaline, sociability. I checked my email before class began. Will, dean of sixth grade, was reminding everyone who taught E period on Fridays that we had to chaperone the Middle School End-of-the-Year Zoom Assembly. It was roughly the sixth email I'd received on the subject. *We will be coming around with smoothies to thank you*, Will wrote. I wrote, *This is mandatory?*

The sixth graders came in and looked with distaste at the *Midsummer*s on their desks.

GILLIAN LINDEN

"I was hoping we'd get new books," Jasper said.

Aurora said, "Mine is falling apart."

"What the physical book looks like doesn't matter," I said.

"It's so hot here today," Lily said. "Can I have a hallway break?"

"Go ahead," I said.

Harlow said, "I found something sexist on page 45."

In my head I heard Agnes say, *Midsummer is a great way to dig into the patriarchy.* I said, "There's a lot to talk about with Shakespeare."

"My dad said he doesn't know why we're reading Shakespeare," said Peter, whose father worked in the college office.

"That's a question people are asking," I said. "It's something we can talk about, together, as a class, whether the problems in Shakespeare outweigh . . . the other stuff." I looked around the room. "Whether there's value in talking about the problems."

Aurora was nodding vigorously, but most of the students looked drifty, bored.

"We're going to start this play tomorrow," I said.

"Tomorrow is the End-of-the-Year Zoom Assembly," said Lily.

"That's after class," I said.

"During class and after class."

"During class, too?"

"It's a double period."

"We'll start the play next week," I said. "We won't write an essay on it. We may not even finish it. Sound like a plan?"

Everyone thought it was a good plan. My relief felt like love— for the students, so amenable; for the middle school office and its

112

double-period assembly; for the English department and its helpful approach to Shakespeare.

"This is a maxim from Goethe," I said. "A German writer. Born
in the eighteenth century."

"I know who Goethe is," Piper said.

TONYA'S OFFICE WAS ON SIX. There was a pansy next to the
door, an outdoor flower, but Tonya failed to consider that, or light
requirements, when she made her selections; she bought whatever
she thought was prettiest and replaced it when it died, and they all
died quickly.

I knocked and a voice, not Tonya's, said, *Come in.*

"I thought we could all speak," Robin said.

Tonya sat behind her desk. She brushed her shirt smooth and
picked something invisible off the sleeve. At the beginning of every
school year she held a meeting on child abuse, making the point
that it didn't have to be *physical.*

"Could be negligence. Could be that the child is afraid.
The child might not know *why* she's afraid. Yes? Those are hard
calls to make."

There weren't enough chairs in the office, and I went again
to the windowsill. There were more plants on the desk, and next
to the chair where Robin sat, a wicker armchair with a beachy
look. At my feet was a ranunculus, its fanning petals only half
in the light.

"I told Tonya she has to give that to me so I can put it in my garden," Robin said. "It's cruel to keep it here, starving really."

Tonya smiled. "Naturally, I don't see it like that."

"Did Jeremy speak to you again?" Robin asked me. "About the bump?"

"He said his head might have bumped into Olivia's," I said.

"Which you saw as a nudge," Robin said. "Understandably."

A nuzzle.

"Yes," I said.

Tonya said, "How would you distinguish between a nudge and a bump?"

"I don't know that I could."

She was watching me. Whether Jeremy had bumped or nudged or nuzzled Olivia might not matter if all I'd seen was that moment of contact, if there was nothing else to add. "I don't know what happened," I said. "It gave me a bad feeling." The plainness of this, the honesty, made me feel like a child confessing to something. I sensed the stirring of an old fear: that I lacked a sense of proportion, and something else, some filter, some critical worldliness other people had.

"Jeremy is no longer working with Olivia," said Robin. "He's gone from *Negative Space*."

"Olivia," Tonya said, as though realizing which student we were talking about. "Did you see the piece?"

"I saw it," Robin said.

"I didn't," I said. "Where was it? The *Post*?" I'd googled the family, found nothing.

"It was only up for an hour," Robin said. "The lawyers got involved."

"About the money? Her uncle?"

"He's just stirring things up." Tonya shook her head.

Robin said, "From what Jeremy said, you'll be able to find out about it in *Negative Space*." She uncrossed her legs and leaned toward me. "Tonya and I were just talking about a piece in the paper the other day. About software used to monitor students taking tests remotely."

"Chilling," Tonya said.

"As you can imagine, it gets a million things wrong." She lingered on *million* so that each syllable was clear. "The technology, I mean."

Tonya said, "A young woman was flagged for looking down— just looking down. Yes? Her professor gave her a zero on the test. She's disputing it, as she should."

Robin said, "Gestures are mostly ambiguous. That's just the way they are. It's possible to see things, read into things . . ." She brushed her forehead, just above her eyebrows. "We know how conscientious you are." This was what Jeremy had said.

"It's a *good* thing to be," Tonya said. "I would've had the same questions in your shoes."

Robin's eyes were on her phone and she was scrolling through something. "*Goddamn it.* Are you chaperoning the assembly tomorrow?"

"Yes," I said.

"You know about the smoothies."

"Will mentioned them in the email."

Robin looked at us both without speaking.

"They aren't good smoothies?" Tonya said.

"They're expensive smoothies. Now Theo is writing to me, upset with me, as if I had anything to do with it. I'm not even getting a smoothie."

"I don't like food that's blended." Tonya moved her hand to a small blue mug, as though to remind herself of something she *did* like. "Well, what about you?"

"Me?"

Tonya let out a breath. "Would you be willing to keep an eye on Olivia?"

I remembered my morning walk with Jane. "Is she close with Erin?"

"Who?" Tonya said.

"Her sister," Robin said.

"*Erin*, yes?"

"Erin," I said.

"Are they close? Is that what you asked?"

"They're different," Robin said. "It's hard to imagine two more different temperaments."

I saw them bobbing toward and away from each other on the sidewalk.

"I don't know Erin," said Tonya.

Robin said, "Which speaks volumes." She sighed, and her eyes drifted from Tonya, to me, to her phone. "I have to sort this out," she said. "The smoothies. I think we're clear, as far as *this* goes?"

"I think we're in agreement," Tonya said. "Yes?"

———

I WALKED DOWN THE STAIRS. Olivia had been moved back into my purview, Jeremy moved out. These meetings felt like clumsy pieces of choreography, as unrevelatory as the pattern I followed when I came home from work, putting my jacket on a hook, leaving my bag on the bench, dropping my keys into the dish. But they weren't without effect. Everything discussed seemed to change. I thought of the apple slices Lewis and I left to dry last summer, becoming thin and papery. *The cleansing power of sunlight.*

Jeremy is sitting at the desk, his arm on Olivia's shoulder. I think: A fatherly gesture. Jeremy leans toward Olivia.

You weren't seeing *things,* he said to me.

I WENT TO THE NONORGANIC grocery store and bought a jar of marinara sauce, rigatoni, and three oranges. I waited on the checkout line as the man ahead of me asked about cottage cheese.

"The kind with large curds," he said.

"We're out," said the checkout person.

"You don't have *any*?" he said.

"No," the woman said. "None."

I said, "You know, there's a place just a couple of blocks down. They always carry that kind."

"I don't have time for *another* stop," he said.

When it was my turn, the checkout woman picked up one

of my oranges, saying, "I'm looking for soft spots. We've had complaints."

I looked at her without speaking, waiting for her to say *Don't repeat this*.

"These seem fine." She met my eyes and shook her head slightly. "You look beat."

"Sorry?" I said.

"It's been a long day, I imagine."

I thought about it. "Not *too* long."

"Drink some water," she advised as I left.

I walked home past the street where I'd talked to Jeremy, the one where I'd seen Olivia, and the blocks were filled with strangers, which gave me a cozy, protected feeling. I smiled at a few of the people I passed and they smiled back. The air was warm and gentle, and very still, but there were fresh smells from the trees, and a few window boxes were beginning to have a lush, filled-in look. I stopped in the hallway of my building to check my face in the mirror, to see if I looked very tired. But I looked fine; I'd seen myself looking worse.

"I HELL," LEWIS SAID when I walked in the door.

"Where did you fall?" I said.

He looked at me quietly. "On the street," Marian said. "Big fall." He had Band-Aids on his palms, and he pulled up his pants to show me more over his knees.

I put on water for the noodles and poured the sauce into a pan to heat up. "Can I make my own salad?" Lewis asked.

"Me too," Jane said.

I brought out cutting boards, butter knives, peppers, grape tomatoes. A few years ago, I'd read about the abuses of the tomato industry and come to believe that buying a tomato of unknown provenance could be as bad as buying factory-raised meat, something I also did, on occasion. "I only eat meat from small farms," Charlie once said. "Meat from animals that lived happy lives." But Lewis and Jane preferred processed meat—hot dogs, sausages— and I usually had no idea where that food came from. Chicken cutlets were hardly better. Chickens were social animals; I'd read about one who was a therapy animal. I remembered pounding away at chicken breasts the other night. I thought, *I should stop eating meat. I should take all the energy I've put into sorting out Jeremy and use it to get Lewis and Jane to like beans.*

I said, "Those are very small pieces, Lewis."

He was turning his cucumbers into a pile of light green bits.

"Lewis is better at this than I am," Jane said.

"I'm going to just leave the tomatoes whole," Lewis said.

We ate the noodles, Jane rinsed her mouth with salt water, and I clipped Lewis's nails and brushed his teeth while he stood in a trance in front of the television. Nicholas was at the office and I took both children into the bedroom, lying first in Lewis's bed, then Jane's.

Lewis said, "How is your head, Mama?"

"Oh I forgot to go to the doctor," I said. "But it doesn't hurt at all."

Lewis went to sleep on his back, his body above the blanket, so that nothing was touching his bandages. I checked my email from Jane's bed and found a message from Dorothy to faculty, staff, parents. Darya had been fired. In the eliding language of the email, she was no longer employed at the school. I read it twice, trying to think what could have happened. I wrote her an email—*hey, checking in, are you ok?*—and immediately received an automated reply; the email address didn't exist.

Jane shifted irritably as she fell asleep. Her toenails scratched me and I pushed her away. "Mom," she said, "this world is made out of mysteries."

"What?" I said. "What did you say?"

"It's a song on the otter show."

LATER, IN MY BED, I said to Nicholas, "If Darya can be fired, why not Jeremy?"

"Who is Darya?" he said.

"Never mind."

He put his phone underneath the pillow. "*Who* is Darya?"

"The movement teacher. Everyone loves her. So how come she gets fired and not Jeremy?"

"There's no reason to fire him if he didn't do anything wrong. He says he bumped her head by accident."

"He does say that." The room was dark, with pockets and corners that were completely black, as though they were openings into a limitless darkness. Except, I thought, there was that donut question. My eyes kept closing. I wasn't sure if I wanted Jeremy fired.

"Of course he was lying," Nicholas said.

"I think so. But why do you think so?"

"You'd remember bumping heads with someone. It doesn't happen often."

"It wouldn't take you a day to think maybe that's what happened."

"Especially not in this environment."

"The lie is the worst part."

"You have to hope it's the worst part." He paused. "My pain is back." Nicholas had *roaming* joint pain since he'd had COVID. He'd been to a rheumatologist and a neurologist and, due to a misheard voicemail, had spent a weekend believing he had a condition that had a 50 percent mortality rate over three years. But he didn't have that. The pain could be dehydration. It could be arthritis. And it could be that he had something new, something that had yet to be understood, described, named.

"Get the hot water bottle," I said.

"I just want to sleep."

"It makes me think of those workplace harassment videos we watch. They always focus on *women* harassers."

"Women can harass men," Nicholas said. "Women can harass women."

"Yes, but how often do you think it works that way compared to the other?"

121

"What does this have to do with anything?"

"I'm saying how is it the woman who gets fired."

"You don't know what she did." He was massaging his fingers, one by one. "One thing is, your job is secure. If they fire *you* now, it will look like retribution."

"Except I only have a one-year contract. I was never officially hired. Jeremy is supposed to tell me about next year, and I've just been *waiting*."

"You always find out late," he said. "This happened in my office. Brian accidentally harassed this girl—"

"Woman."

"Woman. Now she can never be fired, and she should be. She made it through the COVID layoffs and everything."

"Accidentally?"

"He thought he was sending the email to someone else. Brian should be fired, too, for like a million reasons." He put his earbuds back in.

I woke in the night and my hand touched the cold, silky surface of Nicholas's phone. I carried it to the bathroom and placed it on the very edge of the counter, where there was a good chance one of the children would knock it to the floor; it might even end up in the toilet.

FRIDAY

I WOKE UP when the sky was gray, with small openings of pale blue. The trees outside still looked velvety. I brought my cactus and laptop to the table. We had other cactuses in the apartment, which were part of Nicholas's collection. There was a very tall cactus that was dry and hollow. It seemed to have died sometime in the last month, quietly, like the nerves in Jane's teeth. And there was a vine-like cactus covered with snowy needles, which gave the children splinters. But this cactus had been given to me before I'd even met Nicholas. It was eighteen years old, and thinking about this—and about it moving with me from one apartment to another, in its round, very heavy stone pot—gave me a feeling of wonder, and stirred a protective impulse. No one else liked it. Nicholas said it looked like a hand with too many fingers, and Jane said it was wormy. I had put it on the children's windowsill, where the morning light was strong, and Lewis immediately asked me to remove it. When I looked at it, I didn't see fingers or worms, just its stubborn perseverance.

"I woke up," Nicholas said, coming out of the bedroom.

"I can see that."

"What time is it?" He rubbed his face. "What are you doing?"

"It's still early," I said. "This is eighteen years old. Think about that."

"Oh no," he said, "I'd prefer not to." He disappeared into the bathroom and I heard the faucet start.

Nicholas had an early call and the morning was calm. Jane sang show tunes in the shower, stomping her feet for emphasis. Lewis shouted *I'm awake* from his bed. He told me that he'd had only one dream and it wasn't frightening. "We were watching TV. That's it."

I went into the bedroom to change shirts. "Is your video off?" I asked Nicholas.

He clicked a few times in an exaggerated way and gave me a thumbs-up. "But be quiet. I have to talk." And then: "I do hear your point, Ian. And I have relayed your point to the client. And it has been dismissed."

OUTSIDE, THE AIR WAS ACRID. "What is that?" Jane said.

"You smell it, too?" I often caught smells—usually bad smells—the rest of the family didn't pick up on, so this was reassuring.

"I smell it," Lewis said.

We stopped at a bakery on the way to school. Jane ordered a plain roll and Lewis a small ham and cheese sandwich. The people at the counter were talking about a fire across the river. An entire building gone. "What building?" Jane asked.

I said, "A building far away."

The children sat on a metal bench outside the bakery. Lewis said, "This is the best sandwich in the world," but he only ate a few bites, and gave the rest to Jane. "Next time I'm getting this," she said thoughtfully, speaking to herself.

We dropped Lewis off with the floaters. One child was sitting in a stroller with a long cast on his leg, and a withdrawn expression. Lewis gave him a cautious look, and went to stand by the gate.

At Jane's drop-off, conversation was about the fire. One of Jane's classmates lived next to the building, and the family had left their apartment in the middle of the night. Someone was googling pictures of the flames, passing around her phone.

"Wait, they live over *there*?" asked a mother who always wore suits to drop-off. I had never in my life worn a suit, and at this point, I reflected, I probably never would. "Did they change the district again?" she said.

"I bet it's closer than where we live," a father said.

"They probably started here and moved."

"We notice the smoke," someone said, "but what about the West Side Highway? It's doing worse, all day every day."

"What's the highway doing?" Jane said.

"He's talking about pollution from cars," I said. Jane caught her breath and pulled her mask up over her mouth. "Jane," I said, "that's nothing new. Did you hear him? All day, every day."

She looked at me, frowning.

"The point is, it hasn't hurt us *yet*, right?" I thought again of Jane's cells, dusty and . . . But no, I thought. The body is meant to deal with impurities. Jane's cells are *fine*.

I WALKED TO MY SCHOOL, in and out of the scent of smoke. A few years ago my apartment had filled with a rotten, insinuating odor, and the super, who eventually found the source in a burnt pot handle, had talked to me about the patterns of smells, the unexpected places they would accrue and linger. "And obviously," he said, "they can get stuck in your nose." Now, with COVID, many people had the opposite problem: no sense of smell, for months. But Nicholas and I hadn't lost our senses of smell.

I stopped outside the school doors to check my email. Jenny Berardi in the communications office had written to say they were monitoring air quality in and around the school. *Air filters are running*, she wrote. *As always.*

I took the elevator to the rig room.

"I WOKE UP SLOWLY," Eloise said. "I snuggled my pillow. My pillowcases came from a monastery in France and sometimes, with my face pressed against one, I heard the monks praying. I didn't believe in god, but I knew I was a sinner. I wasted money, paid no attention to my child. I liked to stand in front of the mirror. I was so beautiful. I hugged myself, and my arm felt very soft. I must have fallen asleep in my mink."

"I know what the animal is," Daniel said.

"Let her finish," I said.

"I'm almost done," Eloise said. The papers in her hand, printed front and back in a small font, suggested otherwise. Ten minutes later, the character was still in bed, thinking about a wrinkle beginning near her chin.

"I hopped to the floor. My body was very light, but there was something wrong with my balance. I was probably just hungry. I was glad to be touching wood. I sniffed the floor, rolled on it, walked up to the mirror. All I saw was something furry, like a baby bear. It was attractive, I thought I'd keep it for a pet. When I moved my hand, the animal moved its paw." She stopped. "That's it, that's the end."

We clapped and Rosie filled her Zoom window with trumpets and kittens with hearts for eyes.

"That was great, Eloise," I said. "The stuff about monks?"

"You're thinking about indulgences, right?" Caleb said.

Daniel said, "It's a mink."

"Yes," said Eloise. "It's a woman who turns into a mink."

Eloise's mother was thin and pretty, and I once saw her wearing fur, which I'd assumed was fake. "Well, great," I said. "Really enjoyable to listen to."

"The description of the bed," Luca P. said, "made me tired in a good way."

Caleb said, "I'm not an old woman and I don't believe in sin, but I related to the character."

"Old woman," I said. "Was the character meant to be old?"

"Old enough to have a child," Eloise said. "Not *young*."

"OK," I said. We'd had six readers—two birds, a wolf, a fish, a dog, and the mink. All the scenes ended with the characters thrown out of their homes or dead. The mink's experience with the mirror was obviously a form of death. If the piece hadn't been about her mother, it would have been good material for Eloise's narrative. "This was thought-provoking," I said. "Thank you all."

I WENT OUTSIDE TO GET a break from my mask before the Middle School End-of-the-Year Zoom Assembly. The smoke smell was mostly gone, but I could still catch the edge of it, maybe just the bit that was trapped in my nose. I sat on the steps and took out my phone. Olivia walked past me. I saw her pause, look back, and retrace her steps.

"You missed class," I said. "Where were you?"

"I had a meeting with Tonya." She was wearing a T-shirt that stopped above her navel. She didn't have an obvious eating disorder, like some girls in the school. She was small, without any visible muscle tone, her bones lightly padded. I thought of how soft hands used to be—still were?—a sign of wealth. In *some* ways, Olivia led a comfortable, pampered life, like most of my students. She tossed her hair away from her face with a bit of a flourish, and looked at me with her mismatched eyes.

I said, "What about your animal piece?"

"I haven't finished it yet."

"There isn't much time left."

"I know." She seemed to hesitate. It had become a harshly bright day. The sun moved through shadows on the sidewalk, spangling it like sequins.

"It's been a hard year, hasn't it?" I heard myself using some of Jeremy's words from yesterday.

"Yeah," Olivia said.

"But you're doing OK?"

"I guess so."

"Yeah?" I paused. "Will the summer be a break for you?"

"Yeah."

I wanted to ask: *Did he nudge you? Did it feel like a nuzzle? Was that all, or was there more?* But it was as difficult as speaking in an unfamiliar language. *Olivia, has anyone been making you feel uncomfortable? Maybe under the guise of taking an interest in your well-being?* Put this way, *I* might be the first person to come to her mind. I said, "I want to make sure you aren't avoiding class for any reason."

She shook her head. "No, I'm not."

Her expression had become more opaque, and I felt as though I were trying to untangle a knot by tugging hard at one end. I said, "I didn't realize you were on *Negative Space*. Will you do it again next year?"

"I think so."

She began to shift her weight from foot to foot, preparing to leave. I said, "You have a piece in it? A story?"

"I tried to pull it, but Jeremy said not to."

"Who?" I said.

"Mr. Newlin." She looked at me with composure.

I said, "And it's about?"

"What?"

"The story. What's it about?"

"A man who gets in a fight with his family about inheritance, and starts hanging around his sister's house, harassing them."

"Harassing?"

"The sister has a kid, a boy, and the boy has a babysitter, and the man gets together with the babysitter, who's a lot younger than he is. He uses their relationship to get into the house." She paused and laughed self-consciously. "Every time he picks up the babysitter, while he's waiting for her to put on her coat and stuff, he takes something from the house, while the boy is watching. He steals things. Right in front of the boy."

"That's eerie," I said. "Sounds good."

"I was thinking of the abnormal psych exercise you told us about."

"The one with the silverware."

"Yeah." She was fiddling with her phone. "So I put that in, and then I was thinking about some other stuff I put in."

I said, "It sounds like you've been able to, in spite of everything—" But I didn't want to start talking about silver linings, so I said, "You're an excellent writer."

She looked at me with interest. Even students who dismissed most of what I said listened closely when I praised their writing.

"And you liked *Negative Space*? It was a good experience?"

"Yeah."

She didn't seem different. She'd always been reserved, poised to get away. I said, "I'm looking forward to your story. The one for this class. What animal are you writing about?"

"A crocodile," Olivia said. "A man who turns into a crocodile."

I thought, *A predator.* "What's the difference between a crocodile and an alligator? I can never remember."

"I don't know," she said. "They all look like dinosaurs."

"What about the guy? Is there something that connects him to the animal?"

"He's old and rich. He's mean. I'm still working it out."

"Be sure you finish," I said. "I want to read it."

I WENT TO TONYA'S OFFICE on the way to the Zoom assembly. "Come in, come in." Tonya pointed to the wicker chair. It had a soft cushion, comfortable looking, and I thought of the bird's nest from the other day.

"I spoke to Olivia," I said. "She said she missed class because she had a meeting with you."

Tonya smiled. "We did have a meeting, but not during your class."

"I thought so. She's been doing that all year."

"Not just to you. Well, there aren't many classes left she *can* miss. Yes?"

I said, "She told me about her piece in *Negative Space*. Sounds like fact and fiction."

"I guess that's usually the case." Tonya had several thin chains around her neck and she touched them one by one, cycling through some private ritual.

"It was money with her uncle, right? Nothing else?"

She dropped her necklaces. "Oh, I can't discuss it."

"There was this one part about a babysitter. I wasn't sure."

Tonya said, "There are so many people involved in this."

"She called Jeremy *Jeremy*. I can't remember if all his students do that."

"Maybe." She smiled, and I had the feeling, again, that I was missing a sense of scale, that I was being placated, like a child. "I'll look into it." She stood. "You should know Olivia has a lot of support, inside and outside the school."

I turned in the doorway. "What's going on with Darya?"

"Well," she said. "Can't discuss that, either." She opened a drawer of her filing cabinet and didn't look at me again.

THE ASSEMBLY DIDN'T REQUIRE much from me outside of my presence, and endurance of the conditions in the rig room. The sixth grade filed in—my class and a couple of students who weren't in my class—and they all started to complain loudly about the heat. It was hotter than ever, hotter than it had been for the ninth-grade class. What was *happening* here? I told Lily and Jasper to sit by the computer and adjust the volume as needed, and when the grade deans appeared on the screen and the dean of seventh grade said, "I'd like us all to meditate, for a minute, on what we love about middle school," I let my attention wander.

Olivia has a lot of support, Tonya had said. Inside the school, who was supporting her? Robin? Tonya? *Jeremy?* Maybe Erin. I saw them walking down the street, bumping against each other, playing. I tried to picture Erin's face, and couldn't. Instead, I saw Olivia, her brown eye, her closed, almost reproving look. Robin said, *It's not a student's job to communicate.* I thought, *A different person could have drawn her out.*

Irene appeared in the doorway with a young woman, one of the middle school office assistants, wheeling a cart with the smoothies.

"Wow," Irene said, "it really is hot in here." She hung back, looking irritated and uncomfortable, but the assistant walked in.

"We wanted to let you choose," she said, making deliberate eye contact with me. She had an engaged and intimate way of speaking, a projection of confidence and something like hospitality.

"But this is our last stop," she said. "Top floor, tucked away. All we have now is this kind." She held up a cup and looked at it. "Strawberry?" She took out a long white receipt. "Oh look, there's ashwagandha in it. That's supposed to be good for all sorts of things. I don't suppose you have trouble sleeping?" She smiled. "Here you go! We have to run. Sorry about this heat! But it's almost over."

"Really?" I said. "The assembly is almost over?"

"Not the assembly. The *year*. So close." She shook her fist, like Jeremy.

"Come see me before you leave today," Irene said.

"WELL," I SAID, "that was terrible."

"It did go on." Irene was behind her desk, which was plywood, its eddies and whorls bringing to mind a topographical map. On one corner was a shiny black telephone that looked incapable of transferring calls, old fashioned, pretty, and impractical. Irene had placed an elbow on her desk, lightly drumming her arm with the fingers of her other hand. She seemed to have deep reserves of energy and attention, to give whatever she was doing just the right amount of each.

"Marty," she said.

"Yes." Marty—the student who was always eating. During the assembly he'd been dipping his hand into a crumpled paper bag. It no longer struck me as a problem.

"The scones and the video games."

"Oh," I said. "I don't care about the scones. The video games—of course that isn't a great habit for him."

"Next year maybe we won't need tablets in the classrooms."

"Yes."

"You look tired," she said. "I heard you fainted."

"I was just hungry. You know what's going on with Olivia?"

"Some of it. I had some involvement with that family a few years ago."

"You know about her uncle?"

"Tonya mentioned him." She frowned at *Tonya*. "Her dad is awful. Between us."

"Yes."

"I prefer Erin. Olivia was an unpleasant child."

"She was?"

"What's happening now?"

"Whatever it is," I said, "and—can I say this?"

"Of course," she said. "Why can't you?"

I told her the whole thing.

"YOU SAW THIS ONE MOMENT." Irene spoke with her hands, not the way Robin did. She cut the air into sections, picked things out of it, swept through it as though she were wiping crumbs off a table. She organized and made sense of things, and she pantomimed how she was doing it.

"Yes," I said.

"He says it was nothing, there was nothing in that moment."

"Yes."

"Robin and Tonya appear to believe him."

"Yes."

"You don't."

"No, but I'm not sure that matters."

She looked disappointed.

"I mean, I don't know what he was lying about. Whether it was a momentary lapse or calculated. Or more."

"I really don't know Jeremy well," Irene said. She was quiet, as if trying to bring him to mind. "We've worked together so long, and I've never gotten to know him. He's here. I'm here." She held her hands out and apart, *here* and *here*. "I did get to know Olivia a little, as I said, and she's untrustworthy."

"Really?"

"I'll tell you," she said, lowering her voice, "I've heard her eye is *just fine.*"

"The brown one?"

"Oh, I don't know." She moved around in her chair, appeared annoyed at the question. "But if you'd come to me saying she *told* you something, I'd be skeptical." She looked out the door as if she were waiting for someone. "But that isn't what happened. You saw it."

"Yes," I said.

"But you can't be *sure* what you saw."

"Not sure," I said, "but not unsure enough."

"I understand. But now you've told me and Robin and Tonya—and Jeremy. He knows you saw him nuzzle her, if that's what happened."

She was saying that the telling was an action; it had changed things for Jeremy, even if nothing had *officially* changed.

"Yes," I said. "But Jeremy doesn't exactly seem contrite."

"Maybe he believes in his innocence."

"Yeah."

"Maybe he *is* innocent."

"Maybe."

"But he has eyes on him. I think you've done what you can." Her tone was distant, as if I'd been describing a difficult but not particularly interesting problem in mathematics. Her eyes moved to the door again and I started to leave.

"What's happening with Darya?" I said.

Irene spread her hands, palms up.

"Why did she get fired?"

"Can't say."

"I thought everyone liked Darya."

"I adore Darya."

"That's what I thought."

"Everybody adores her."

"Yes."

We were silent for a moment, contemplating Darya.

"I can't imagine her being out of bounds in any way."

Irene shrugged. "Well."

"Really?"

She met my eyes. "Emails. Could have happened to anyone."

"Inappropriate emails?"

She straightened some papers on the corner of her desk. "Emails to students late at night. I don't think the *content* was inappropriate."

"That was it?"

"There was an email she wrote to Will or someone, but she sent it to a parent. Accidentally. She was letting off steam. But the parent she sent it to . . ."

"Was it about Ivan?" I said.

Irene smiled. "It was a mistake."

"Something like that happened in Nicholas's office, but they didn't fire the guy. I guess it depends on who receives the email."

"Yes." She raised her eyebrows. "And what the email says."

I was almost in the hallway. "And what people do about it?"

"Yes," said Irene. She was turned away from me, reaching for the phone. "That too."

I PRESSED THE BUTTON FOR the elevator and could hear it hum and rattle, but it never came and I took the stairs. I walked slowly. The stairs were usually filled with students—jumping on top of one another, dragging instruments and athletic equipment, heavy backpacks stuffed with books and snacks. But on Fridays the building emptied quickly, and the stairwell felt airy. There were odd sounds, footfalls, but it was hard to tell if they were in front of or behind me. I crossed paths with a small boy holding a violin case, his expression determined, as though he were just beginning the day when everyone else was leaving. On the fifth floor, the lights were flickering, but windows let in the sun, pale and watery, so I could see well enough. An eleventh grader I'd taught ran ahead of me, shouting *hello* without looking back, the way a person might stand over the Grand Canyon and yell *echo*. And Olivia walked past me, appearing in the dimness as though summoned by my ruminations. She was moving quickly. I said, "Have a good weekend," and she turned at the sound. Her face was expressionless, and she didn't say anything. I thought, *Does she see me?* But then she smiled and was gone. After Olivia came a tall man, also moving fast, maybe a floor behind her. It was Jeremy and he was staring at his phone. He patted my shoulder, murmured, "Have a good weekend," and kept going. "You too," I said, watching him. In the lobby I saw him leave the building, but when I stepped outside there was no evidence of either of them.

IT HAD GROWN HOTTER SINCE the morning, and the sun hit my skin in a way that felt pointed, as though it had been waiting for me. I didn't have news about Jane, which meant she'd remained in school for the duration of the day. Jane's teacher wasn't unlike Elodie's mother. She loved Jane, embraced Jane, but you wouldn't call her a *physical* person.

My phone rang, and it was my friend Jessica. I sat on a bench in front of an apartment building. "I've been needing to talk to you," I said. I told her about Jeremy and Olivia, Robin and Tonya. I told her what I'd seen on the stairs.

"You think he was *following* her?" Jessica was a public defender. She was sure of her opinions, and was regularly struck by the stupidity and vanity of the people around her, including, from time to time, me.

"Not really," I said. "I don't know."

"The problem is you saw just the wrong amount. It's too bad you saw anything."

"Too bad for me, maybe not for Olivia. Maybe it's good for her that I saw something, and said something."

"Like the subway ads," said Jessica.

"My worry is," I said, moving over, trying to fit into a sliver of shade, "he's not going to change. Because I did see him, and reported it, and nothing happened."

Jessica said, "I'm going to get you tuna and cucumber." Nora, Jessica's daughter, was a friend of Jane's. Jane occasionally said Nora was her best friend. "But," she sometimes added, "I don't really like her."

"Sorry, I have to go," Jessica said. "We can talk more later." She paused. "It doesn't matter what he thinks about it. If something happens again, they'll have to get rid of him."

THE WOMAN AT THE FRONT DESK of urgent care pointed me to a screen where I could check in. I put my hand on a scanner, and the computer couldn't find me, even though I'd been there before. I was glad they didn't have my handprint, but it took a while to type my name and address, my insurance, and then there were more questions, page after page: Did I smoke and had I ever smoked? What about drinking? Drugs? And did I have a heart murmur, cancer, diabetes? Was I the recipient of an organ transplant? How about my mother and father—had they had strokes? What about *their* blood sugar? When the answer was yes, you had to explain, briefly. It was the catalog of *sufferings and miseries* I'd ticked through at countless doctors' offices, but the insensitive touch screen made it all take longer. I left out some conditions that were small, or irrelevant, or would require a lengthy explanation, and a couple that I just didn't want to think about, and I assumed everyone faced with these lists did exactly the same thing. By the end of it, I felt detached in a way that was almost pleasant, as though I'd jumped into a cold lake and had a little buffer of numbness all around me.

There was a woman sitting by herself in the last row of chairs, a history teacher who had started at the school the same time I had. We'd been friendly during our first year, sitting together in New Faculty Meetings and having lunch a couple of times, but I'd barely seen her since the beginning of COVID. I put my things down a few chairs away from her and said, "Jamie, hi."

She looked at me and smiled, and gestured for me to come closer. "I think we're already exposed to each other. School germs. What are you here for?"

"I fainted and hit my head," I said. "It's fine now. It doesn't even hurt."

"I heard about that. I didn't know it was you."

"I was just hungry."

"I'm glad you're OK. I guess?" She looked around the office as if to say, *So why are you here?*

"I'm fine. Just a checkup."

"OK, good."

"How about you? COVID test?"

"No. I think I broke my toe. I stubbed it." She gently lifted her foot to show me her untied sneaker. "I'm afraid to take my shoe off."

"When did that happen?"

"Just now. Like an hour ago. I hit it pretty hard on a desk."

"I've broken a toe," I said. "They wrap it up with the toe next to it to stabilize it. It's called a *buddy toe*." She looked at me blankly. "I'm sorry. It's so painful."

"It brought tears to my eyes!" she said. "I wasn't *crying*, but my eyes just filled with tears, like chopping an onion."

She was around my age and dressed in an enviable way; she could make unremarkable clothes—trousers, T-shirts—look like they were made especially for her. Even her unlaced shoe looked, somehow, just right. "Can I ask you something?" I said.

She waved her hand, gestured to the empty waiting room.

I said, "Do you know Olivia?"

"Yeah," she said. "She's going to Brown."

"What?"

"She got in off the waiting list. Maybe her parents will calm down. You know them?"

"Olivia's parents?" I said.

"Really on-it people."

"Not that Olivia."

"Oh. You mean the one in the lower school? The singer?"

"No," I said. "I don't know who that is."

"Apparently she's quite something."

"No, the ninth grader," I said.

"Do you mean Oona?"

"Olivia," I said. "Erin's sister."

She put her hand to her mouth. "Are you sure?"

"Yes."

"I didn't know Erin had a sister."

"She does," I said. "A ninth grader. Olivia."

"Oh, hold on," she said. "The one with the eyes?"

"Yes," I said.

"OK," she said. "No. I don't know her."

We sat for a few moments in silence. I saw Olivia in class, head down; saw her walking with Erin; saw her expressions, which came and went in a flash. I thought, we might as well be teaching at different schools. I had the slipping feeling in my stomach—a presentiment of panic—that would happen sometimes when a jar was closed so tightly I couldn't twist it open; a sense of weakness.

Jamie said, "Erin was fine. Quiet." She thought for a moment. "Can I ask *you* a question?"

"Sure."

She turned to me. "Did you get a smoothie?"

"Yes," I said, and her look of disappointment cheered me up.

"*How?*" she said. "I saw them going by, but the girl said I couldn't have one."

"They were a reward for chaperoning the assembly."

She seemed to consider it. "Probably not worth it."

"Probably not," I said.

THEY BROUGHT ME TO a spacious room in the back of the clinic, and the old man—my favorite doctor—shined a flashlight into my eyes.

"You said this happened on Tuesday?" he said.

"Yes."

"And you've had a headache since then."

"On and off. I get headaches, apart from this. I have young children. And all the Zooms."

He seemed to smile.

"What do you think?" I wanted doctors to reassure me, maybe give me some medicine. I didn't want anyone to become *too* interested. But this man was like Wendy, the school nurse. It seemed unlikely that anything I said would produce a strong reaction in him.

"It's expected, if you fall on your head, to have some pain." He gave me an admonishing look. "It's not, I assume, the worst headache of your life?"

"Oh no." The office was neat, not beautiful or ugly, but rigorously dull and muted. "I do have some light sensitivity."

"Really."

"Not much."

"And everything looks fine, and you're saying you *feel* fine."

"Mostly. People keep asking me why I fainted." I realized no one *had* asked me this.

He said, "Why did you faint?"

"I was very hungry."

"So there it is." He sighed and sat back. "I think you should come back if something changes."

"OK," I said. "I tend to notice things."

"Yes."

"So what would be a worrisome change?"

"Well," he spoke softly, "if the pain gets worse, if your vision—"

"Wait. If you tell me symptoms, I'll start getting them."

"Yes. Just come in if you feel like it." He smiled in a benign way. "When I see you again, we can touch base about your head."

"So you don't think I'm about to drop dead?"

"Oh no," he said, patting me on the shoulder. "Not with those vitals."

I STOPPED BY THE FARMERS' MARKET before going home. It was slowly coming back, and now, in addition to apples, there were stands for honey and mushrooms. I loved the mushroom people, evangelists who would tell you the medicinal properties of this or that variety, and the best way to prepare them. They often clipped off a sample of a mushroom I'd never tried and slipped it into the bag with my usual royal trumpets or blue oysters. But I didn't feel up for a long conversation about mushrooms and went to the apple stand to pick up Mutsus for Jane. She only liked this one kind, and could eat it in enormous quantities, and I put as many as I could comfortably carry into a plastic bag, and went to pay. The woman at the cash register was eating a donut. "Trying to de-sugar myself," she said. "It isn't easy."

I walked home past the school, the most direct route. Sometimes, to give myself more separation, I took a circuitous path, but today I felt so saturated with the school, its teachers, its students, passing the *building* wouldn't amount to much. And it was a good building, old and solid. Sometimes art teachers would bring children to the street outside to draw, or there'd be a music class with instruments. A few times I'd seen lower school science classes, a group of students just older than Lewis, with magnifying glasses and notebooks. I could understand, then, why parents were so eager to send their children here. The year I'd started, I dreamt that it was snowing *inside* the school, which was dark and wintry.

"That means you like your job," Nicholas said.

"Maybe," I said. "Or I like the idea of it."

AT HOME THE OTTER SHOW was playing and Lewis and Jane sat in front of it, mesmerized. Jane glanced at me when I came in and raised her hand casually, as if acknowledging an acquaintance.

"What do you have planned this weekend?" I asked Marian.

"I'm just going to rest," she said. "I haven't been sleeping well."

I put broccoli on a baking tray to roast and defrosted shrimp under the faucet. I asked Lewis if he wanted to help. He didn't. "And I'm not going to eat it," he said.

I steamed rice, and Jane told me about lockdown drills at her school, which had apparently gone poorly.

"A soft lockdown and a practice hard lockdown," she said.

"What's the difference?" I said.

"For a soft lockdown, you freeze." She froze, slightly crouched, fingers splayed. "For a hard lockdown, you sit against the wall. You have to be below the windows because you don't know where the robbers will be spying on you from."

"Stop eating tomatoes," I said.

"Do you have any more questions about the lockdown drill?" she said.

"Why did you think it went badly?"

"The lock on the door didn't work." She picked up another tomato. "Everyone kept moving except me and Freya."

At dinner Jane told Nicholas about the lockdown drills and asked again, "Do you have any questions about the lockdown drill?"

Nicholas said, "Do *you* have questions about the lockdown drill?"

"Yes," Jane said. "What do robbers want to take from the school?"

"Did your teacher talk about that?" I said.

"No."

Three weeks ago, a parent in Jane's class had alerted everyone on the second-grade parent group chat to a post on Twitter encouraging people to come into schools and commit acts of violence—all over the country, in all kinds of schools, including elementary schools. I showed the post to Jessica, to Nicholas. I googled it; it was determined to be a hoax. But what did that even mean, a *hoax*. That the person who posted it hadn't made any *plans*? What about everyone who read it?

Jessica said, "This is going on all the time, on websites we don't read. We just happened to see this one."

"I know," I said.

"They're in no more danger tomorrow than they are any other day."

"That isn't really a comfort."

"The point is, it wouldn't be rational to keep them home tomorrow."

Nicholas said, "I wish we didn't know about it."

Jessica sent Nora to school and I sent Jane, but the woman who'd emailed the Twitter post kept her son home.

"I don't know what the robbers want to take," I told Jane. "Let's ask your teacher about it," I said, buying time.

I LET LEWIS WEAR JUST a diaper to bed. I let him brush his own teeth. I let Jane skip salt water. Lewis and I watched cooking videos on YouTube in the dark while he drifted off. The man in the video was an old, famous French chef with a gravelly voice. He poured cream over some mushrooms. "Not nearly as much fat as butter," he said.

"Do we have cream?" Lewis said. He was lying on top of me, his head against the center of my chest, bone against bone.

"You'd like to make this?"

"No." He rolled off and away from me. "Not really."

"Mom," Jane said as I lay next to her, "is Dad going to start traveling again?"

"Yes," I said. "Soon, but not very soon. Not tomorrow."

"OK." Her breathing was becoming heavier, more rhythmic. Sleep built up in her gradually, like water filling a sink. "I'll miss Dad, but I love you," she said. "I like your cold comfort."

"Why do you say 'cold comfort'?"

"Because your arms are cold."

I closed my eyes with the pleasant feeling that I could fall asleep easily, quickly, and I did, but I woke up an hour later and had trouble settling back down. Little things kept coming into my head. We were low on vinegar, and I wanted to order a warmer lightbulb for the fixture over the table, and I had to go through a notebook I kept to see which of my students were still missing large assignments. I checked my email and found a reminder that I also had to fill out a survey for the high school office. The head of the high school was new—he'd started this year—and he had a passion for surveys and feedback of all kinds. He'd encouraged us to solicit feedback from our students, something I was extremely reluctant to do. Other teachers felt differently.

"I'd want to know," Tim had told me. "I mean, wouldn't you rather find out from *them* than from a parent sending an email to Jeremy?"

"But don't you think it opens the floodgates?"

"Oh, those are already open," he said. "Don't you know that? They've been open for a couple of decades at least."

"But asking them."

"We ask them things all the time. This is just another conversation."

"A different kind of conversation," I said.

"Sure."

"And you don't think they're telling you the truth, do you?" I said.

He laughed. "They don't know the truth."

I'd observed one of his classes when I was interviewing for the job. He was completely at ease, with a self-confidence that seemed to appeal to students.

"They don't know much about anything we talk about," he said.

"But with the other conversations, you correct them. When they're wrong."

"Sometimes I do." He shrugged.

"When it's important."

"Important?" He was silent, as if wondering whether anything that happened in class could be called important.

"But the feedback," I said, and he looked away, irritated, as if I were being ill-mannered. "You don't do anything with it?"

"What would I do with it?" He still had that look on his face, and it encouraged me.

"I mean nothing *happens* with it? It doesn't change anything?"

He shook his head. There was something else in his expression, not confidence and not irritation, something like patience; he was treating me like a student. "The feedback changes things," he said. "It does do that."

So I'd asked my classes what they thought of the workload. The ninth graders, naturally secretive and alert to hidden motives, imagined this was an opening to criticize them. They shut down, becoming very quiet and saying only that the workload was fine. But the sixth graders saw no reason why anyone wouldn't want their opinions. They jumped right in, offering strongly felt and contradictory suggestions. The workload was too much, too little, and the longer assignments came at very inconvenient times. For creative writing they were desperate for more opportunities to just *freewrite*, just *express themselves*. To do this they needed more and better prompts.

"Very helpful," I said, and I didn't ask for feedback again. Let the parents send their emails.

I BROUGHT MY LAUNDRY BOOK to bed and read about the removal of difficult stains—barbecue sauce, blood. The words remained firmly in place, the sentences coming one after another forcefully and clearly, illuminated by my attention. I thought, *Why can't my mind be this sharp when I'm teaching?* I thought, *I need to switch books so at least I learn something worthwhile.* But I didn't switch books. I picked up my phone and ordered a number of detergents, and a little scrub brush, and a square bar of soap to be rubbed into what the book called *phantom stains*, and then I put everything away and closed my eyes. I squirmed in bed for a long time. I was too hot, too cold, and trills of anxiety ran through my stomach and chest. But eventually I fell asleep.

SATURDAY

I WOKE UP and untangled myself from Jane, who'd climbed into bed at some point in the night. I shoved her toward Nicholas, someone else to sleep against. I was still tired, with a feeling of sand in the back of my throat. I pressed my fingers to my cheeks and went to the living room. The sun was just coming up, and the edges of the clouds were torn and yellow. I went to my desk and looked at a maze Jane had drawn a couple of weeks ago.

"Mom," she'd said, "will you do my maze? It's a maze where you exit the maze."

"No," I'd said. "I'm doing the dishes."

She asked again a couple of minutes later.

"Not now," I said.

"Mom," she said, "will you do my maze?"

"I'm eating breakfast," I said. "I need *three minutes* in my head. Can you give me that?"

She came back. "Will you do my maze?"

I said, "Give it to me."

"It's a maze where you exit the maze."

She'd drawn a square with two little gaps in its border, on the left and the right sides. The first gap opened to a path that led to a smaller square, completely self-contained; there was no way out.

Beyond that there were a couple more looping paths. One led out of the maze, but there was no way to enter that path from the entry path. The exit path began out of nowhere in the center of the maze.

"I can't do this," I told Jane. "I go in and I'm stuck."

"It's a maze where you *exit* the maze." She took the pencil from me and drew a line into the maze, turned around, brought her line around the maze, came back into the maze crossing the border of the maze and a couple of her paths, and exited the maze through the gap on the right. "See?"

The paper was creased in a few places and had a dry smudge of something orange—jam—in a corner. It sat next to a water-color of Lewis's from school, which was very beautiful. Pools of rose and green, darker in some places, lighter in others, over-lapped in rounded shapes that reminded me of ocean animals—seals, whales. Jane's maze wasn't beautiful. It didn't look delicate or strange, like some of her other drawings. It looked like it might be the creation of a younger child: a few lines and scribbles without any discernible organizing principle. The drawing was a mirage. You *exit* the maze.

Jane came out of her room and loped toward me, one shoulder higher than the other, grimacing and rubbing her eyes. She often woke up this way, as though her surroundings were a rough sur-prise, as though she had to remind herself how to walk, as though each morning she really was re-*born*. She went into the shower and I heard her singing.

"Mom?" she shouted.

"Are you done?" I said.

"No," she said. "Just checking."

JEREMY HAD SAID HE IMAGINED there'd be a sixth-grade class, maybe a fifth-grade class, maybe a tenth-grade class for me in September. He'd stopped me at one of our end-of-year department meetings and said, "I'll be in touch as soon as I know."

I spent the next couple of weeks wondering if I should turn it all down. Just leave the school. Nicholas thought I should, so did Jessica. My mother thought I should stay but only teach one class, and, finally, I agreed with her. My job was an important counterweight to my life at home, with all its tedious chores. It pulled me out of my feelings about Lewis and Jane, which could be so consuming I worried they'd obliterate some part of me; I worried they'd turn me into a wistful, sad-eyed person, a person pining for something impossible, some kind of permanence. I couldn't give up the job yet.

Jeremy called at the beginning of July while I was home with the children. Lewis was playing with my watch and I was teaching Jane how to make a friendship bracelet.

"I don't have *any* classes for you," Jeremy said.

The apartment was humid, but cool. I'd turned the lights off, and the ceiling fan kept the air circulating softly, over and around us. Nicholas's plants were in constant motion.

Jeremy said, "We'll miss you."

"This way?" Jane said. "Mom, this way?"

"Hang on," I said to Jane.

She said, "It's all twisted. The blue should go first."

"Just wait," I said. "I'll fix it."

"Something else may still come up," Jeremy said.

I didn't say anything.

He said, "If it does, you're at the top of my list."

ACKNOWLEDGMENTS

THANK YOU TO David McCormick, Ed Park, Ginia Bellafante, Stefanie Victor, Julian Bittiner, Sophie Pinkham, Ashley Lefrak, Cassandra Cook, Forth Bagley, Mary Rasenberger, Madelaine Gill, Holly Gill, and Eugene Linden, for reading these pages, fielding all manner of questions, offering the soundest advice. That the book found its way to Matt Weiland, who saw its best version immediately, and Huneeya Siddiqui, feels like a small, personal miracle. And I'm grateful to David Feinberg, for his multiple readings and his ear for the comic and ominous.